THE
METAMORPHS

By
S. J. BYRNE

I0541414

ARMCHAIR FICTION
PO Box 4369, Medford, Oregon 97504

FOR CENTURIES EARTH WAS BEING INVADED...

Shahn was one of the last survivors of the Nrlan, an advanced people with psychic powers, who destroyed their home planet and most of their own race to prevent the spread of the Metamorphs to other worlds. Bred from a chrysalide, a Metamorph was a monstrous creature, evil beyond compare and human in appearance. The ultimate horror for Shahn's people was that they themselves, when biological circumstances were right, transformed into these horrid beasts—beasts with a taste for human souls. After his wife was slain, Shahn resolved to destroy the Metamorphs once and for all, and keep them from contaminating the Earth. His only hope of success lay in the Earth woman, Lillian. But could he trust her?

Be prepared for a wild novel that challenged the limits of the sci-fi field when it was first published in 1957. It's a tale that former Amazing Stories *editor, Ray Palmer said would establish "Stu" Byrne as one of the giants of the science fiction world. "The Metamorphs" is a forgotten sci-fi classic that will challenge your thinking processes and at the same time excite and entertain you.*

FOR A SECOND COMPLETE NOVEL, TURN TO PAGE 135

CAST OF CHARACTERS

SHAHN
He was the lone survivor of a 200-year long journey, but after landing on Earth, he found the alien horror from his past.

VRULNUS
Leader of the Nrlani race, he was thought to be the one with the power to stop the Metamorphs—but was he alive or dead?

ROSPOR
He could rule an entire planet if he could get the blueprint for a special weapon that could tear the soul out of a human being.

CHARLES DALANEY aka MENLOR
He was in a trusted position, guiding the Nrlans to safe bases. But he had a dark secret he didn't want known—just yet.

DR. NIMR LANIS
This Doctor was more than happy to help out Nrlans immigrating to Earth. But what were his real motives?

PEARL GORDON aka NRLANI
Her main role was to be the distraction…the cookie, so to speak. But she fell in love with her objective!

LILLIAN HAMMER
As a reporter she was ready to find out everything she could about Shahn—and what she found was her worst nightmare!

CHAPTER ONE
A Quarantine For the Promised Land

BENEATH the shell of consciousness, dreams and memory combined in Shahn's struggling mind. After two hundred years, he was stirring out of suspended animation.

*   *   *

Nrlan!

Graveless is Nrlan, world of the dead great past. It drifts a nebulous cold cloud of death and ashes down the shoreless sea—emptiness where once were dreams and love and laughter—and dark despair.

Beloved mate, wearer of my own scar of *san,* Sralna, she of the summer moons, who died in terror. San Dialnis, Valley of the Jansi Light. We walked together there, Sralna and I heedless of the *Change…*

Rospor, so tall and inhumanly thin, with his deep, dark eyes and glasslike nose—standing there weaponless yet menacing and demanding.

Sralna, with only her sleeping robe, awakened by the intrusion. He hated the uninhibited gaze of Rospor.

"The *Khal* has entrusted you with the complete details. You must comprehend them, as you are his chief disciple. I want the *sarniall* weapon."

"The weapon belongs to Vrulnus, *Khal* of Nrlan. You know it is the only hope of our kind against the Metamorphs." He placed a protecting arm about Sralna, his mate in *dialnis.*

"Nothing can stand in my way, Shahn. You will draw me the plans of the *sarniall* or suffer the consequences."

"You idiot. Even if I should prepare them, do you think you could escape the power of the *Khal,* who alone stands against the Metamorphs? If they do not fear him, why do they send you to me, instead? Go ask mighty Vrulnus himself."

"I am not alone..." The strange note in his voice chilled them with the shock of its implication.

"Do you mean—that you, a human serve *them?"*

"Yes, you fools. The only logical answer is to cooperate with the enemy. The Metamorphs depend on us for their continued existence as a species, since they evolve from us yet cannot reproduce. Can't you realize that our own power of procreation is the currency for bartering? In exchange for collaboration they will give power undreamed of. That is why I am commandeering one of your star ships tonight and taking off with a load of Metamorph chrysalides for the new world. They have assured me of the power to rule any planet, provided that I obtain the secret of the *sarniall,* and I intend to get it."

He leaped at Rospor and was met with a staggering blow. Before he could recover, Sralna screamed. The room began to darken. Or rather, a *darkness* was taking shape in it—a terrible kind of darkness that tried to recall a subliminal memory of deadly existence before the advent of humanity. Latent, pre-natal stimulus-response patterns took over in the presence of that materializing evil, and one tended to shrivel up and curl away from it, seeking the darkness of the egg in preference to life fraught with this incomprehensible terror. It robbed the mind of reason and will before the steam-roller impact of wild shrieking fear. At first an amorphous shadow, it quickly assumed the proportions of a jet-black, faceless man—a Metamorph!

Above Sralna's screams he could hear Rospor's laughter. "Hurry, Shahn before it takes her life."

The sheer madness of desperation threw him upon the shadowy thing, and his hands were numbed with cold when he tried to take hold of it and drag it from his mate. Color drained from her beautiful face along with the precious miracle force of life itself. And her hair... Visibly, it was turning ashen gray.

"Stop," he cried out. "I'll do it. I'll give you the plans—anything."

"No you won't!"

It was great Vrulnus, the *Khal,* himself, on the threshold—Vrulnus, leader of the race, the single human force in the universe to oppose the nemesis. Ah, precious man. Only one *Khal* such as he may be born in a thousand generations. He stood there, towering above Rospor, his gray eyes ablaze with anger, the twin scar symbol of the *Khal* gleaming on his broad brow, in his hands a glowing *sarniall*—the only completed one in existence. As he activated it, the room spun around and around...

To obliterate *them,* Nrlan was destroyed. Vrulnus had offered his people this terrible solution—or the unspeakable alternative.

Thus the star ships. Year after year the flat, circular ships leapt interstellar chasms broader than life...

* * *

Shahn opened his eyes and focused them at last upon reality. At first this reality consisted of a section of the ceiling, criss-crossed with conduits and air-lines. Ingrained stimulus-response patterns struggled against conscious awareness. Mental defense mechanisms sought to reject the evidence of catastrophic events, which lent truth to his tortured memories.

This could have been the ceiling of a subterranean apartment on Nrlan where they hibernated during perihelion near the solar reservoirs and the incubators, while on the surface world the plants and trees folded in upon themselves and exuded a heat-resistant coating.

Soon the summer years would come when they would emerge. He remembered the thousands of lakes and lagoons, the soaring mountains, the landlocked seas with their myriad islands and the four moons that governed their life—the Moon of Jansi, under whose light only the generation of the procreators might walk—especially in that land set apart for lovers, San Dialnis…

"Sralna," he cried, sitting up suddenly and looking about him in the crypt-like ship.

Instead of Sralna, he saw the long row of hiber-bunks upon which the passengers lay. Grinning skulls stared back. The others had not survived the suspended animation.

They were dead, long gone with the memory of tragic Nrlan—and Sralna.

Why had he alone survived? Was it that his people had seen in him their future *Khal;* in the event that Vrulnus should not come through? He had been laid here while yet unconscious. By whose careful hand had his body been prepared for the long, dark journey? Perhaps his beloved teacher, Vrulnus, himself. And now where was *he?*

Shock held him incapacitated for an unmeasured time while he sweated coldly, alone in the unknown abyss of Infinity. Where was he? And to what avail? Could even the genius of the *Khal,* himself, have penetrated the vastness of lifeless worlds and pinpointed their objective accurately—and could his miraculous machine creations hold to such a tenuous orbit?

Yet the fact that he was conscious now gave proof that automatic relays were at work after all these years. Sensitive thermo-couples atop the low dome of the star ship had been activated by some nearing sun. Mere microamperes of current were creating magnetic fields in tiny solenoids, which were tripping powered relays. The ship was awakening, too.

As the only surviving passenger, certain responsibilities now devolved upon him. He stirred himself, at last, and entered the observation dome. Through the leaded, polarized visiports he saw again the ponderous star-walls of the universe, but without Sralna this mighty symbol of the Immortal Plane assailed him again with an overwhelming sense of loneliness. Why not go out the airlock and embrace oblivion?

Why not? Ah, there was the essence of the ageless dilemma—finite self versus the instinct of ethnic survival. This ship belonged to his race. It represented a part of the Exodus, a unit among thousands, but a precious symbol of their heroic bid for life. It had to complete its mission. There was work to be done.

Moreover, the haunting premonition pursued him that if Vrulnus had not come through, then he, as the great one's last living disciple, must become *Khal*. To him the survivors would look for guidance and salvation.

But no! Futile thought. Vrulnus was indestructible. He *must* have survived, and even now was taking charge of their new life in the promised land ahead. Shahn forced himself to hold to this and nothing more.

First of all, the tapes should be read. Probably for years now they had been recording occasional messages transmitted from the bases set up on the new world by the earlier arrivals from Nrlan. Owing to variations in velocity of the various ships over the long period of time required for the journey, it had been foreseen that some would arrive many years before the others. Since his own ship had been among the last to leave, he wondered how long the first to arrive had already been settled in the new world and what their transmitted reports would reveal.

But before he listened to the tapes he used the electronic telescope. The new world was the third planet of this chosen system. Even at this great distance he could make out its disc, and detect the promising color of chlorophyll green and see the welcome white of suspended water vapor.

"Ship 763," blared the speaker system, which was patched into the receiver circuit. *"Nrlani Base N-1 calling ship 763. If any survivors hear this, reply immediately."*

He looked dumbly at the speaker. From that distant world he was looking at, one of the voices of his own kind had reached out through the abyss of space and addressed him.

"Ship 763." The message was repeated, while Shahn marveled at it. To hear someone else's voice, speaking to him in his native Nrlani tongue…

He flicked a transmitter switch and answered. "Ship 763 to Base N-1. This is Shahn of Vrulnus Base. What are your instructions?"

There was an answering silence, which puzzled him at first until he remembered that radio waves were limited to the velocity of light. At his present distance from the new planet it would require some time for his message to be received and a reply returned. So he busied himself with the tapes to learn what message of hope had been received out of this brave Tomorrow, which his people had wrested from the callused hand of Fate.

Yet, even as he permitted his resilient spirit this slight unfolding of optimistic wings they were suddenly clipped short. He had not wished to spin the tapes all the way back, so he had listened in at random and heard—

"…It has not been fully determined whether or not Rospor succeeded in reaching Earth. If he did land here and establish his Metamorphs, there is as yet no indication of it inasmuch as the Metatmorphs thus far encountered on this planet may have come into being as the result of varying other circumstances, such as a failure to commit suicide before metamorphosis owing either to cowardice, amnesia, or indeed that same degenerate lust for power, which deviated Rospor from the course of human allegiance. Suffice it to say, our curse of old has been brought to this innocent world, and the responsibility develops wholly upon ourselves to…"

He shut it off abruptly and stared through a visiport at distant Earth. A slight film of perspiration was on his skin. Lumps of muscles along his jaw tightened, and his deep-set black eyes gleamed bitter hate under heavy brows.

"Metamorphs!" he exclaimed, his voice almost breaking under the stress of his emotions.

After all the dangers and the torment, after the sacrifices and the antiseptic obliteration of a planet greater than Earth, *they* had gotten through to contaminate this last horizon of hope. And Rospor. He should have killed him that last night on Nrlan. Curse him and all his kind on Earth.

He lunged at the port, his hands spreading across its cold smoothness as though he would cup the Earth in his palms like a wounded bird. "Thanks to Ao," he cried. "I am still young, and Vrulnus was my teacher. I'll fight. I'll track them down. I'll build a *sarniall.*"

The thought of Ao gave him pause. Strange, after the death of his world and at the end of this terrible journey, he should still cling to the thought of Ao.

When Nrlan was destroyed—what of its moons? What of great, dark Gral, and the eternal light of Ao that mystical entity, which glowed always in the black disc of the farthest moon.

Legend had said many things of Ao. Vrulnus, the *Khal,* had intimated much more—that it was even the secret of the greatness that once was Nrlan's prior to time-misted cataclysms of the buried past.

The thought that even this eternal thing was gone into the gulf of Yesterday accentuated his sense of futility. He sweated and raged silently within, as he gazed ahead at the innocent world to which his kind had brought a plague worse than death.

"Ship 763," blared the speaker. His message was being answered. *"Base N-1 to ship 763 and operator Shahn of Vrulnus Base—welcome to Earth! Long has your arrival been awaited, Shahn. Stand by for course coordinates, which will bring you to N-1. We have succeeded in keeping our presence a secret from the inhabitants, as originally planned, so entry into the atmosphere is required precisely over the base, itself..."*

Shahn could not resist an emotional outburst. He flipped on the transmitter switch. "How do I know you're not a Metamorph?" he demanded.

Minutes later, the answer came back.

"You don't. But that goes both ways, doesn't it? Our base task force will intercept to make sure you land where we want you..."

Shahn hurled one more burning question. "The *Khal,*" he called. "Did *he* come through?"

After what seemed to be too long a wait, the reply returned, cold and factual.

"Vrulnus, *Khal* of Nrlan—is dead."

Shahn stood looking at the inanimate speaker as though it were alive. At last he clenched his fists and shouted, "It's a lie!"

But he suddenly thought it wise to say no more. Vrulnus, greatest of *Khals,* was indestructible. Surely he was there, hiding out for reasons of his own. And Shahn would find him.

If not—and if Vrulnus were truly dead—then by all the old laws *he* was *Khal.* If this latter were true, then he was no longer subject to their instructions.

A *Khal* must initiate his own plans if he were to guide his people...

CHAPTER TWO
Contact

CHARLES DALANEY opened the front door of his portentous home in the Hollywoodland Hills. And suddenly he regretted it. The rough looking character outside filled him with suspicion.

"What do you want?" he asked.

"I am Shahn of Nrlan" was the simple reply—and it was not in English.

Dalaney tried not to tremble or perspire or to faint from sudden vertigo. He struggled mightily to compose himself. From a black immensity deep as light years and centuries old came these words, blasting into his consciousness with staggering impact.

"I—ah—I'm afraid I don't—"

"Cut it out, Menlor. Let me in. If you doubt my origin, there are always the *tests.*"

Shahn shouldered his way into the luxurious home, dark-visaged, bearded, lean and hungry. He held the collar of a worn coat against his throat. An old felt hat shaded his dark eyes.

"But—it's incredible," exclaimed Dalaney, closing the door reluctantly. "Two years ago you announced your presence while still in space. You never landed at the Mackenzie River Base."

"A good thing," muttered Shahn. "Base N-1 was wiped out by a Metamorph raid a few days *prior* to my arrival."

"By the Eternal. I did not know… Not N-1 Base, too?"

Shahn doffed his hat and a curly mop of black hair fell upon his brow. His eyes bored into the other's. *"Didn't* you know? I wonder, Menlor."

"Please—the old names, the mother tongue—we have eliminated them here."

"We? Who is *we?* Vrulnus has disappeared. In his absence, *I* am *Khal."*

"No *Khals,* my friend. All that is dead."

"We shall see. But just now—let's have the tests."

Once the study door had been closed and locked, making the room soundproof, Dalaney finally managed a nervous smile.

"Won't you sit down? You look hungry. Maybe—"

Shahn looked at Dalaney warily. "The tests," he insisted. "Remember?"

"Oh yes. The tests. Might as well get them over with."

Shahn's dark eyes narrowed sternly. "You may be a thirty year veteran here," he said, "but you're careless. What if I were—"

"Don't worry." Dalaney's soft looking face hardened and his eyes went cold. *"They* would never enter here. Your shirt, please."

Swiftly, Shahn removed his coat. Then he lifted up his shirt, exposing his abdomen. Dalaney looked and was reassured. His visitor had no navel.

"Plastic surgery," he remarked. "Doctor Lanis is our man. Now for the eyes."

He procured from his wall safe what appeared to be a small penlight, while Shahn stuffed his shirt back in place. Then he pointed it at Shahn's unblinking eyes and turned it on.

It was as bright as a photographer's flood lamp and concentrated into a sustained pencil beam that would have blinded an ordinary pair of eyes for hours or perhaps days. Dalaney watched the pupils become pinpoints, almost disappearing entirely before a thin, translucent inner lid slipped down over the cornea.

"As long as we're being so routine about this—" He offered Shahn the test-light.

The other's mouth tensed. His eyes stared into Dalaney's. He fumbled hastily with the light and finally brought its piercing beam to bear. Instantly, Dalaney's pupils closed to pinpoints and the filmy inner lids appeared, which were characteristic of the Nrlani.

"Anything else?" asked Dalaney, patronizingly. "I could arrange the heat test to give conclusive evidence of the extra *purnial* gland, or give you a stethoscope so that you could tell my heart is in the center of my thorax, or give you a strength test or demonstrate our different sense of time. Or perhaps the high frequency test of the auditory. I have a signal generator. Now after all, Shahn—"

Shahn's strong chin trembled. He fumbled with the light, dropped it, then grasped Dalaney's face in both his hands and thrust his fingers into his eyes.

"What the hell?" Dalaney recoiled with a mercurial swiftness, which would have been impossible for an Earthman, striking the other's arms away.

"I believe what I can *feel*," shouted Shahn, suddenly overcome with rage and frustration. He clenched his fists and cried out through his teeth. "They are everywhere— infesting the Earth with a plague worse than death. You know they have the upper hand by now—so what was the use of everything we did?" He flung himself onto the leather divan, his face buried in his hands, *"Sangrulna diancas nal chiodun diniktla tlaliari..."*

"Shut up," Dalaney snapped, coldly.

Hastily, he went to his liquor cabinet and opened it. He probed at the back of it, up behind a drawer, and soon he extracted a small, black case.

The hypo served to settle Shahn's nerves to where Dalaney could reason with him.

"How many of your group came through?" he asked him, as he mixed two highballs.

Shahn straightened up on the divan and pulled himself together. His outburst had been one of frustrated strength rather than weakness. He looked around the room as though seeing it for the first time. One wall was all books, a flawlessly normal selection, from history and philosophy to sexual behavior and gardening.

"I was the only survivor," he answered.

Dalaney stopped mixing to look at him wonderingly. On his own ship, everybody had lived including his young wife.

"Don't look so surprised. It was almost twenty cycles of time—two hundred Earth years. What do you expect?"

"You were—with your mate?"

"No," sullenly. "You ought to remember the last days—how we left Nrlan. We were lucky to be passengers at all. Who but the most fortunate could hope to be with his immediate family? But just look at the sacrifices, the tremendous accomplishments, the planning and hopes—for *what?*"

Dalaney did not choose to answer. He came over and handed Shahn his drink. Then he sat down beside him and they seemed to share a common vision—a golden nostalgia and a black revulsion.

After a long silence, Shahn laughed bitterly. "What did the Earthmen first call our ships when they saw them?"

"Flying saucers."

"No. That's understandable. But, what were some of those other things?"

"You mean—hallucinations, weather balloons, atmospheric reflections, beer bottle caps—"

"Yes. That's it. By *Vrulnus.*" He deliberately emphasized the sacred name, pretending not to observe a flicker of what might have been dark resentment in Dalaney's eyes. "If they could only know the background of those ships—the terror and the striving and war and destruction and heartbreak—the incredible night of waiting, gliding in deathly sleep across the star roads, dreaming of survival only to smash against an unyielding barrier of futility."

Dalaney studied his guest in calm deliberation. "And your own ship, Shahn? What did you do with it?"

Shahn's eyes searched Dalaney's cautiously. "I tried to hide it, but somebody got to it."

"Burned, eh?"

"Yes. *They* don't want our kind to escape them—ever again. Each of us is a precious link with immortality—for *them.*"

"That's why the Nrlani are scattered and hard to find, Shahn. They are the constant prey of the Metamorphs, who must force them to procreate. If the Nrlanian species dies, so do they."

Shahn finally finished his drink and got to his feet. He began pacing the room.

"Now to business," he said. "I have searched for you, Menlor, because you are the nephew of Vrulnus, and before N-1 Base was eliminated you were attached to it here as regional director for the West Coast area of the North American continent. You handled secondary orientation before things broke up and all Nrlani had to take cover. There are few I can trust in these latter days, but you I will *have* to trust."

"Shahn—" Dalaney shook his head. "In the old world, you would have been *Khal.* Here—forget it. The day of hope has passed. You have seen the newspapers and heard the commentators. Metamorphs have taken over public office in the guise of the favored leaders of Earth, and these poor Terrestrials don't know what's happening."

Shahn whirled about, his eyes blazing. "My people have not solved this problem—therefore it is all the more evident they need their *Khal.*"

"And what would you do, Shahn—if we hailed you as such?"

"Before considering that the question is, where is Vrulnus?"

Dalaney shrugged. "He is dead. You know the facts by now. He is reported to have landed at the Siberian base years ago, and the Metamorphs jumped him. He was destroyed, utterly."

"Did *you* see his body? Did *anyone?*"

Again, Dalaney shrugged. "You demand that we hope in the midst of darkness. Hope is too much of a burden, Shahn. We can only live our secret lives—"

"In as much luxury as possible, eh?" Shahn interrupted. "You know, Menlor, you're not doing so badly. A splendid home, a nice manufacturing business, two cars, servants. You even have children."

Dalaney's face colored momentarily. "Under ordinary circumstances your deadly inferences would be a gross insult, Shahn, but I suppose it's natural that we should all be suspect until the proper association and passage of time develops confidence." He regained his composure and took Shahn's glass for a refill. "My children are adopted. My wife is Nrlanian, admittedly, but she has submitted to sterilization."

Shahn watched Dalaney in brooding silence. It was a silence, which Dalaney sought to minimize by busying himself with the preparation of the highballs.

Finally, he returned to the divan with fresh drinks. "Let's get off these discussions for tonight," he said. "After a good supper and shower and shave, I want you to meet Doctor Lanis. When you are all fixed up, we can talk, in a few days, perhaps. What you should do for your own happiness is settle down, work for me, and—perhaps raise a family."

"What are you talking about? No Earthwoman could conceive by a Nrlanian male."

"I'd find you a suitable Nrlani."

"But—"

"I know. My own school of thought approves of avoiding the metamorphosis by not procreating at all. However, there is always the old way—at the age of sixty or so…"

"Sleeping powders or gunpowder. I know. That's the way that doesn't work. One puts it off until it's too late, and when the green sweat comes along, the instinct of self-preservation becomes accentuated. From then on, even before the chrysalis stage, one is committed to metamorphism. No—this is not for me. I seek Vrulnus. He was working on a study of the metamorphosis. He told me that, given time and sufficient research he might find a cure."

"I did not know that."

"There are many things you do not know…but *I* do."

"Perhaps, Shahn, if you could build the *sarniall*—you might yet be *Khal.*"

Shahn smiled a cold, lean smile. "The day I build it, my single bid for life will be gone. *They* know where I am. They leave me alone, waiting for me to put the *sarniall* together. They know the weapon is not the answer now—not unless it is mass-produced and backed by an army. They would take it by force of numbers, and my value to them would have ceased. But the very possibility of the *sarniall* haunts them. Vrulnus conceived of it, and if I can build it, then someday someone else may do the same. They must figure out its principle so that they may invent a defense for it, and so they want the *sarniall*, and they wait for me to show my hand. The time is not yet ripe."

"And may never be," sighed Dalaney.

"What I want," growled Shahn, "is to find Vrulnus, or *Rospor.*"

Dalaney laughed. "Rospor is an equal legend. No trace of him was ever found."

"Don't be so gullible. For all I know, he may be the false *Khal* of Earth by now."

Dalaney looked away, examining his fingernails. He raised his brows. "And you would fight single-handedly against such forces?"

Shahn's eyes fixed Dalaney's with a cold stare. "The only thing that may be taken from me is my life. Sooner or later, I'll have to snuff that out, anyway, to avoid becoming a Metamorph. So until that time I'll risk every second of life to fight against Metamorphs and their collaborators—and to find either Rospor, or Vrulnus, or both."

"I see…"

Shahn wondered just exactly what Dalaney meant, and the latter left the brief statement unqualified, as though it were self-explanatory, which it most definitely was not. In fact, Dalaney had tossed out a few cryptic remarks at the height of his emotions, but Shahn figured they were booby trapped and left them where they lay…

CHAPTER THREE
Dialnis

THE GIRL, who had once posed as a nightclub singer, had changed her name from Nrlani to Pearl Gordon. After three years of experience in Dr. Nimr Lanis' offices she had become an efficient receptionist and assistant. Shahn learned at the start of their acquaintance that she was of his own race. This was brought about by Dalaney's announcement to her concerning the nature of the operation.

"Navel," he had said, as though that could explain everything. Then he added, superfluously, "Plastic surgery."

"I understand," she answered, while sweeping a more than casual glance over the patient's face and figure.

"How do you understand?" Shahn demanded to know.

Her brown lashes lifted. She gave him a significant look as she pointed to the ceiling with her ballpoint pen. "Have you forgotten the Light of Jansi so soon Shahn?" There was a sad amusement in the sly twist of her half smiling, half-parted lips.

The regular light was out. An Earthman would have found himself in darkness here. A tube of the special light rested in the bottom of the bowl, shining through, filling the room with a light and a color unknown to Terrestrial eyes. It was also a very subtle light, engendering a series of delicate and personal thought associations. In the old world, two marriages were necessary for final confirmation of permanent matrimonial status. The first was Jansi, and under the Moon of Jansi Shahn and Sralna had achieved the miracle of *dialnis,* which is mental rapport—a unity of being. Once *dialnis* was reached, the second and final marriage was consummated. It was then the female wore the sacred scar of *san.*

Coming into a room illuminated only by this source of light was a perfect test and a proof that everyone able to see was Nrlanian. But it could also be a trap sometime or somewhere in the future, because the owner of the trap could be a Metamorph, a black, faceless, inhuman fiend, hypnotizing him, making him believe that he was looking at a normal man, or a personal friend. That was why he had lunged at Dalaney and *felt* of his eyes, back there in his study.

But Metamorphs never tried to make any normal man think he was looking at a young girl of Pearl Gordon's obvious attractions. They could not transmit the illusion of that exciting psychological interchange in look and manner, which was as unknown to them as were rainbows to blind men or the patter of rain to the deaf.

"I was of the Lanlai," the girl explained. "Under the influence of the Moon of Lanlai I dreamed, as a girl, of entering the time of Jansi." She reddened slightly, watching him. Or was she testing him? To a Nrlanian it was very frank conversation, as the Jansi generation were the procreators of the race. "Strange," she hastened to add, "that I should enjoy the Light of Jansi only under such synthetic conditions—here in the presence of the great Shahn, himself."

Shahn was forced to become more aware of the girl since she had touched upon such a personal subject. She was young and had soft wavy brown hair and large, subtle brown eyes. She was lithe without tallness, stylish without severity, and intelligent without complacency. Moreover, her lips were as feminine as her smile was comprehensive. And she was a Nrlani.

"Shahn," said Dalaney, at his shoulder, "this is Doctor Lanis."

Somewhat in a daze because of the girl, Shahn found himself looking at a very friendly man with a black goatee and a bald head. His light blue eyes were the most disarming part about him.

"Welcome to Earth, Shahn," said Doctor Lanis, with surprising heartiness. "I'll have you disguised in no time so that you could pass a Terrestrial medical examination anywhere."

As the two older men led him into another section of the suite of offices where there was standard incandescent illumination, Shahn took another quick look at Pearl Gordon, who still sat at the receptionist's desk, doing nothing at the moment. Unless he could construe her pensive surveillance of his departing figure as being strictly in the line of duty, she did not often see a newly arrived *young* Nrlanian male.

One thing he knew for sure. Nrlanian women were not any different from Earth women when it came to instinct, and the most basic instinct was procreation. Here, after the long, cold ride, with their home world destroyed, young and unsterilized Nrlanian women could be irresistibly attracted to a healthy male of their own species, for they could conceive by none other. Yet that very instinct was being outlawed because the curse of mutation must die.

The *Metamorphs* must die.

Even if young love and a woman's instinct must be violated, death to the accursed enemy came first if the secondary matter of life, love and the pursuit of happiness were to become anything more than a long lost dream...

*   *   *

It was one of those little Italian places. Western style, with knotty pine paneling, a log fire, checkerboard tablecloths, candle light, martinis and pizzas. The small dance orchestra was taking a recess, as were most of the waiters, inasmuch as only three tables were occupied. This being a resort town, and the month being May, the first wave of the tourist season was expected momentarily.

"It isn't like home," said Shahn, "but it's a fair substitute, I think, considering the circumstances."

He was looking between two candlesticks at Pearl. She had a persistent way of looking at him from under her lashes, and he was haunted by the thought that she was withholding something from him, because she was anything but demure.

She was too sharply intelligent, too exhilaratingly frank, to be diffident or shy. It was as though she were parrying or avoiding something by repartee and mannerism that she hoped he would never discover.

"It was a wonderful thing for me that Mr. Dalaney and the Doctor finally influenced you to give up a hopeless struggle and settle down to a normal existence." She paused, then asked, "Are you happy?"

"It is the customary thing for me to ask *you,*" he answered. "Sweetness, don't laugh at me. I know it may seem silly, since we weren't able to marry in our own way, to even imitate the process here. In fact, all Earth marriages are merely equivalent to our first stage of matrimony."

"The Jansi stage," she murmured sadly. "And here there can never be the final stage. Not *dialnis*. I could never wear your scar of *san.*"

He smiled. "You can't go around wearing the *san* on Earth. On Nrlan the *san* would be considered a beautiful and enviable symbol of permanent attachment, but here your unsuspecting terrestrial acquaintances would ask you what hit you between the eyes to make such a peculiarly symmetrical scar."

"John—" She pronounced his assumed name softly, as a compromise with reality, so that it almost sounded like Shahn. "Why did you rush so into this marriage?"

"I saw no reason for waiting. Here you were, and here was I. There is a lot of loneliness and a long, dark night of memory to wash away."

"Seriously—was it rebound? I mean—you told me about—"

"Get off that, Pearl. You know it wasn't that."

"Well, how about this one, then? Our racial situation here constricts life. Is this quick marriage a form of—rebellion?"

"Say! What is this? After all, there may be a much simpler explanation. I want you to be happy."

She reached out and took hold of his hand. "Of course I'm happy," she said, smiling. "At least there is one parallel between this and Nrlan. They have honeymoons here, which is not too different in its meaning from our Valley of San Dialnis."

The fact that *San Dialnis* had no really adequate translation made him moody. You had to have the racial memory and peculiar stimulus-response pattern of the Nrlani to grasp its true significance. In an attempt to capture the spirit of this lover's hegira of his own world, he had insisted that they take a two-week honeymoon, and it had landed them in the Russian River country of Northern California.

"We shall speak here neither of the future nor of the past," he told her, lifting his glass.

As they looked at each other, their smiles slowly faded.

"Oh, John," she exclaimed, searching his eyes. "I'm glad you're happy. Terribly glad."

"Say! What's all this concern about *my* happiness? What about you?"

She turned her head abruptly to look at a crowd of tourists coming in the door, and at the musicians returning to their stand. Then she looked back at him with a peculiar little smile.

"Let's call for those pizzas. I'm starved."

They drove down the highway toward the sea, high above the river valley. There was a high concentration of cirrostratus that cast a fairy scrim of enchantment across the apparently racing moon. Isolated stands of pine stood out on the great slopes, limned with dull platinum, and nobody seemed to inhabit the world but they. It was an old, old world, sad and beautiful with myriad memories of unnumbered lovers who had seen and loved it.

"The Valley of San Dialnis," Shahn muttered. "We only need a temple or two up on the hills to make it real."

He had parked the car on a tremendous bluff above the sea, and they could look back at the delta of the Russian River and a curving expanse of its course beyond, where it came out of the forested hills. A soft, steady wind from the ocean pressed against them, just cool enough to remind them this was night. It tossed part of Pearl's brown hair across one side of her face as she took hold of Shahn's hand and surveyed the moon-washed scene in silence.

"You have been there," she said, finally, "but I have not. What happened to your mate—your first one—you told me so little."

He filled his lungs with the invigorating air and was silent for a while. Then he answered, "What happened on the other side of time and space should be forgotten."

"I'm sorry." Her hand pressed his, remorsefully.

"She died," he added, unexpectedly. "On Nrlan. That's all far away and—"

"All right," she exclaimed softly. "I made a booboo. Let's forget it." She kissed him lightly on the cheek and pulled him toward the edge of the bluff that looked out over the sea.

The sea fanned out away from them, blending imperceptibly into the darkness of the sky like a titanic launching ramp that pointed into the bottomless void of the universe. Nowhere could they turn without sensing the heaviness of their racial memories. The awareness, deep down in their minds, that their kind was rare, like a few grains of sand blown into the infinite deserts of space, drew them irresistibly to each other.

"Water, water, everywhere, and not a drop to drink," Shahn muttered.

She looked up at him. "Rather incongruous, to say the least."

"It's what the shipwrecked mariner is supposed to exclaim. It's equivalent translation into Nrlanian would be, I think—" He spoke slowly in their own tongue, saying, "A haven of life lies here at the end of the terrible journey, and we have found it—but to die."

"*Shahn!*" Her arms went about him in a swift, desperate movement, her head pressed tightly against his chest.

He held her to him in a crushing grip, glaring out over her shoulder at the trackless sea. "All this cannot be," he cried. "Our race—the glories and the power of Nrlan—the golden age of the *Khals*. Why do I yield to such an impossible circumstance when my blood cries out for retribution? When every fibre of my being shouts: Strike back! Call your people to arms! Without their *Khal*—they die."

She kissed him on the mouth to quiet him. "You are my *Khal*," she said consolingly.

With a fierce abandon, he suddenly enfolded her deep in his arms and kissed her hair, then lifted up her face to his and found her lips again. She responded with a feverish haste, as though their passion were a clandestine, forbidden thing that was soon to be barred from them forever.

"Did anyone ever tell you, Shahn of Nrlan," she whispered tensely, between her teeth, "that you are a very fatal man? Your magnetism is a *sarniall* no woman could resist."

* * *

Later, they discovered a path, which led them to a grass-grown ledge under the shoulder of the bluff. The ledge faced the ocean, and beyond its rim a cliff dropped almost perpendicularly into the faintly roaring surf two hundred feet below. The moon was just finding the ledge, and they knew that it would be almost morning before it sank beyond the sea. They sat there wordlessly for a quarter of an hour before Shahn broke the silence.

"Have you ever heard any news concerning Vrulnus?" he asked.

The mention of this great name pulled her abruptly out of her subjectivity, and she turned to look up into his eyes. "No one knows if he lives," she said.

"In him alone is our only hope for survival. I wish I knew his whereabouts or the Earth name he assumed."

"How can you be sure he has not been victimized by the Metamorphs already, as Mr. Dalaney claims?"

"To believe that he lives is mental defense. To abandon all hope would leave nothing but the void of insanity."

"Shahn," said Pearl. "Tonight the subject is morbid. Do you mind?"

He kissed her and she clung to him again with that indefinable desperation she had demonstrated before. The moon reached its zenith and still found them there on the ledge, long after conversation had failed them as an adequate means of expression.

I am closer to you than I have ever been
We are one, you and I

"Shahn!" She sat up and looked at him as though she were going to scream.

"Of course," he replied calmly. "What else is it? What else could it be?"

"Dialnis," she exclaimed. "I have experienced *dialnis*—in this far world—and with you! Oh, Shahn—"

He tried to hold her again, but she shook her head, suddenly bursting into tears and pushing him with her hands against his chest.

"I had begun to fear it would happen," she cried. "But I needed you so—I thought I dared take the chance. It was only rebound for you, I thought, and for me—"

He held her at arm's length and looked at her face. "What do you mean—you *thought* you dared take the chance?" he asked her, fiercely.

"I'm their decoy," she exclaimed bitterly. "Dalaney is a collaborator; and Doctor Lanis is a—you know *what*." Shahn looked at his hands, clutching her arms, and wondered at them. They seemed not to be his. He was of stone—suddenly cold and devoid of nerves. Petrified.

Then, with almost invisible swiftness of motion, he was on his feet, and she with him, his fingers digging into her flesh. "That cherubic, red-cheeked little blue-eyed man, Lanis—*a Metamorph*?" He shook her. "You? His instrument?"

"Yes. Yes," she cried, completely out of control now, her face streaked with a flood of tears, her hair in her eyes. "He maintains one of the major incubators under special acceleration. Oh Shahn. Shahn. Forgive me. You are the first one to bring *dialnis*—I had hoped against it."

"How many others," he shouted. "Tell me!" His eyes impaled her with almost murderous intent. No wonder, he thought that Dalaney had not resisted their marriage plans and Lanis had been so merrily enthusiastic.

"Dozens, out of his office, but they were just—"

"I know. I know. Skip it. Skip everything. I should kill you. Why have you become—this *thing* that you are? A prostitute, all right. But not the egg-breeding instrument of a—of a—"

"Don't you *know*, Shahn?" she sobbed. "They have their eyes on you as their most dangerous enemy and biggest prize next to Vrulnus. They know you are next to be *Khal,* but they wanted to tie you down, with myself as the instrument of barter. I could tell you other reasons for this—there are dozens of girls—all Nrlani—doing the same thing on the West Coast, for Lanis' incubation center. Call it mental coercion—weakness, hopelessness—the line of least resistance—but I don't care to excuse myself—not with you. Oh Shahn. *Dialnis.* I never expected it, but you—"

"Shut up!" He slapped her face, several times, hard. "Do you know what I am going to do? I'm going back to kill Dalaney, and then I'm going to assemble a *sarniall*—yes, that's what I said. The weapon of Vrulnus. I am going to destroy Lanis' chrysalis and any others that may be lying around. And you're going to show me where he's got his buried."

She broke free. Before he could stop her she was over the ledge. He saw her go, diminishing moonlit figure, plunging irretrievably toward the pounding surf and the barnacle encrusted rocks.

He stood there looking down. The moon moved in the heavens while he stood there, eyes and mouth very dry, totally alone.

Perhaps he could have spared this young girl's life, he thought bitterly, if he had told her the truth—that he had sacrificed her to an inconsequential Jansi marriage as a ruse to gain her confidence—that he had recognized her as the weakest link in Dalaney's chain of collaboration—that the real prize obtained was the unexpected knowledge that Lanis was a true Metamorph.

As for her experience of *dialnis*—he had also neglected to tell her that Vrulnus had taught him the rudiments of telepathy.

He shuddered, depressed and overwhelmed with remorse and loneliness. She had been so beautiful, so young—

CHAPTER FOUR
Hideout

SHAHN crumpled up his last available cigarette in an ashtray. He had been smoking too much—getting the dry hack in his throat. Coffee, cigarettes, sleepless nights—long months of uncertainty, battling against time and the handicap of not having either references or credentials, living in remorse over the avoidable death of Pearl Gordon, and eating and breathing a mind-ravening rage and hate.

From this single window of his improvised lab he could look out between giant wharf sheds at a slice of San Francisco and see the tugs and lumber boats moving out under the mist-shrouded span of the Bay Bridge—all the peaceful activity of terrestrial life, which was as yet totally unaware of this invisible invasion of forces beyond its control—and his own control, as well.

But he had to fight, in the very teeth of futility. He had to build the *sarniall* before returning lone-handed to Dalaney and "Doctor" Lanis in Los Angeles. The construction of the deadly weapon required money, which at long last, was finally coming in. But there was the rub. To obtain it, he had found it necessary to donate to Earth a forbidden piece of Nrlanian science.

And this shortened his available time, because *they* could now trace him down through the patents applied for by his customer. They would be waiting for him to show his hand like this—any revolutionary piece of science in the world, a suspicious event, a single clue that might lead to their prize. Sooner or later—

Abruptly, someone knocked at the door.

He tensed mercurially, turning swiftly to glare at it. The landlord never visited this property. No one else knew he was here, since he came or left the premises solely by night.

The only mail he ever anticipated—royalty checks sent to him by the Jonathan Corporation people whom he had benefited—was sent to a post-office box. *No one* had his address. This could not be a salesman knocking—not inside the closed warehouse at the private door of his lab.

Whoever was out there had come specifically to see *him*.

"Who is it?" he asked, finally, his pulse racing.

There was no reply. Only the weather-cracked, barren door facing him in enigmatic silence.

He grasped one end of a worn tarpaulin and threw it over the gleaming articles on his work-bench—precious parts of the *sarniall*. He wished to Ao that he had it finished.

The knock was repeated, gently, but with obvious determination and a cunning patience.

Shahn stood still in the center of the room, looking at the door, frowning at the insistent pounding of his heart. Had they found him so soon? Dalaney or his dark master? Or was this an agent from some more important center come to take him captive?

He ran to his desk and procured an old automatic that he had bought from a fence. Thrusting it into his belt, he threw on his coat and went to the door. Eyes gleaming defiance, he took hold of the knob. They'd not take him alive—not even Lanis, himself.

Violently, he swung it open.

"Good heavens…"

The soft, almost musical tone of the voice matched the face and personality of the chic young brunette who stood outside. Her clear, blue eyes were wide with astonishment—her expressive young lips parted in alarm. Then he noticed her hair, raven black, darkly glistening, and copiously long, partly lying across one neatly padded shoulder. She carried a blue leather drawstring purse to match her smartly tailored powder blue suit, and a dog-eared notebook. He also caught a glimpse of long, cool nylons and slim, wedge-heeled shoes before he found his wits—and his voice.

"I—ah—beg your pardon. Just kicked a salesman out of here. Thought he had come back."

"Oh." Those gigantic blue eyes. Not dumb, either. They didn't penetrate—they absorbed.

"Ah—what I mean—were you looking for someone? How did you get in here?"

"Through the door." Those lips were worth a thousand words, expressing three compounded innuendoes at a flash. When he offered her nothing in return, she said, "I hope you are Anthony Meade."

This was his new alias. But— "How the devil—"

"The *Press* has its own peculiar ways of uncovering a story, Mr. Meade," she said quickly, with a perfect admixture of politeness and self-assurance. "I'm from the Star-Express. May I come in a moment?" She flashed a laminated plastic I.D. card at him.

He read the card laboriously, momentarily deprived of his native eidetic faculty of reading pages at a glance. "What story are you talking about? I'm afraid I—"

The girl tilted back her head and laughed so genuinely that it brought a faint smile of response to Shahn's dry lips. "Story," she exclaimed. "You are the inventor of the high-voltage storage battery and you can ask such a question? Why Mr. Meade—you must know you've made technological history. Did you think for a minute that you could hide from your grateful public?"

The Press! Why hadn't he considered this contingency, written a limited secrecy clause in the contract? What if he told her the *real* story? Well—the main point was to give her the brush, as they so aptly put it in English. That white marble perfection of a nose she was wearing could make history, too—the wrong kind—if she persisted in sticking it into *this* business.

She came in, cool morning blue, a breath of fresh air and a rainbow flash of healthy intellect, and she stood there in the middle of his lab—and in the middle of his desolate life.

An Earth girl, the most beautiful terrestrial female he had ever seen. Smiling at him, gazing unabashed at the evidence of his bachelor existence—the dirty dishes in the sink, his unsorted laundry on the cot, yesterday's newspapers on the floor, cigarette stubs camouflaging ashtrays.

Suddenly, he was laughing. It was more nervous reaction than genuine amusement. What a contrast *this* was to all his dark forebodings of a moment before.

But the girl wasn't laughing. She was looking gravely at the gun in his belt, which he had inadvertently exposed to view.

"Don't get any ideas about that," he told her quickly, taking it out and placing it carelessly on his desk in front of the window. "I help pay for my keep here by being a watchman."

Her eyes and her expressive mouth told him she had observed that the warehouse was empty—practically abandoned—but she said nothing. Instead, she walked over to his chair beside the desk and sat down, inevitably crossing her slim legs as she did so. Shahn wondered why Nrlanian women had never discovered nylons—one of the most intriguing and ingenious inventions in the universe.

"I'll ask you a question first," he said.

"Yes?" She smiled attentively.

"I'm curious. How is it a young woman of your obvious attractions has the courage to come to a place like this—an empty warehouse on the waterfront—to interview a strange man, alone? I do read newspapers once in a while, you know."

"But the wrong headlines," she countered, easily. "You're not a tramp, Mr. Meade. You are an accomplished scientist—and my friends at the Jonathan Corporation told me about you. I think any aggression on your part would be directed at something much more significant than a mere female. Now, shall we get on with the interview?"

Insight or coincidence? His aggressiveness *was* being concentrated on something far more significant.

"You have friends in the Jonathan Corporation?"

"I get around. I'm science editor for the Star-Express."

"But they haven't my address here."

"You visit your post-office box every Friday evening. That's enough of a lead for us professional snoopers. Now tell me, Mr. Meade—"

"Your I.D. says your name is Lillian—Lillian Hammer."

"So?"

"Miss Hammer—there can be no interview—not at this time."

She looked away, out at what could be seen of the Bay. Then she turned her head quickly, impaling him with a determined glare. "Mr. Meade, history has an inevitable way of being written. If it isn't me there'll be a long line of others. So why not get it over with? My paper feels its readers would like to know more about you. Do you know who you are? You're James Watt. You have just invented the steam engine and the Industrial Revolution is around the corner. Why, that battery of yours will make internal combustion engines obsolete. It's even the death-knell to smog—and you deny me an interview?"

He smiled. "You omit the fact that such a battery is what the atomic age has been waiting for, also, but—please don't think I'm trying to be coy about all this. Incidentally, how about panhandling a cigarette? I'm fresh out." He sat down on one edge of the desk, leaning over her, aware of a deliciously elusive perfume.

She reached into her purse, but her eyes never left his face. She offered him a silver cigarette case and he helped himself to a Viceroy.

"You're not the coy type," she answered, "and I'm not trying to be facetious. The battery is story enough, but what I'm really trying to get at is something else now."

He exhaled a pale blue smokescreen, but she penetrated it, still studying his face. "And that is?" he queried.

"It's—it's indefinable, but it's there. In the first place, if you'll pardon me, I don't think your real name is Meade—"

"Why not?"

"Your descent, whatever it may be, is not related to such a name. I'm no anthropologist, but I can pick out obvious racial types—Spanish, East Indian, Slavic... You have the facial characteristics of a Valentino, yet you're not Italian. You have a touch of the Western Hemisphere Indian, and yet that's not it, either. There's a touch of the exotic, a sort of out of this world look—and there's such a sad loneliness in you, like the result of some great tragedy—and there's some tremendous emotion motivating you. I wish I knew your *real* story, Mr. Meade, or Mr. Jones, or whatever your aliases are..."

"Miss Hammer, you're in the wrong business. You should be telling fortunes." He did not smile.

Neither did she. Her eyes still concentrated on his. "You mean in this case I struck pretty close to home."

He got up and started pacing the room. "I'm sorry, Miss Hammer. This is getting both of us nowhere. For purely selfish professional reasons I find it necessary to maintain the greatest secrecy about myself at this time."

"In other words, to publish details about you would perhaps—*endanger* you or your plans?"

He whirled about, his face taut. Then he relaxed into a controlled smile. "Let it go at that. I wish I could help you out but I can't. The matter is purely one of professional caution and not at all as bizarre as you imagine."

She looked briefly at the gun resting near her elbow, then back at him. Suddenly, she smiled and got up. "You win this round," she said, "under one condition."

"And that is?"

"Let me wash the dishes."

"Let you—"

He looked at the untidy sink, then back at her, his heavy brows coming together in puzzlement. "But I don't get it."

Before he could stop her, she had wrapped a dishtowel about her slim waist. Her sleeves went up and she was at it, peculiarly silent and industrious about it all.

Dumbfounded but curious, Shahn sat down in his chair to watch her. After a while, he said, "What kind of charity do you call this?"

She removed the towel and began drying the glasses and cups briskly. Finally, she looked his way, a strange little smile on her lips. "Maybe I wouldn't be able to explain it to myself," she answered, "except that—something tells me strongly that you need help. I don't know how to help you. I wish I did."

She finished quickly, stacking the dishes neatly on the sink. She pulled down her sleeves, gave her hair a characteristically feminine adjustment, and came over to the desk for her purse and notebook.

"Thanks," he said, simply, not getting up.

She paused to look at him. "Is there anything—" she began. "I mean, my paper would—"

"Nothing." He shook his head, smiling.

"Could I come back again sometime?"

"As long as you keep me a secret."

"I have a feeling you won't be staying here long."

"Perhaps not."

She backed away slowly. "Well, goodbye, Mr. Meade. Thanks anyway."

"Thank *you.*"

She turned, then, swiftly, and was gone.

Shahn sat there motionlessly, looking at the empty doorway. He knew that neither of them could explain why she had washed the dishes—and a lot of other things too far out on the horizon of comprehension to be defined.

He watched the Star-Express carefully after that, and. although he found Lillian Hammer's science column he could discover no betrayal of confidence. Jonathan Corporation was organizing publicity for release as soon as they could swing into mass production on the high voltage battery, but he knew that by that time he would he ready to strike in Los Angeles. Work on the *sarniall* progressed rapidly now that money was coming in from royalties on advance contracts, which Jonathan had obtained by means of well placed confidential correspondence, particularly with the U.S. Government.

In the midst of his fevered work, one persistent thought had aged him mentally and added few outward lines of care to his already drawn face. He had previously fixed Vrulnus in his mind as his goal—but of late a new thought had inserted itself with increasing insistence. *What if Vrulnus were truly dead?*

This possibility presented him with a very pointed fact, like the sword of Truth pressed against his heart. He, Shahn, chief disciple of Vrulnus, would then be the only last living hope of his kind.

To place the burden of hope on another such as Vrulnus had been a relief—but when he considered that he might actually be carrying upon himself, alone, the entire burden of responsibility for his race, owing to the teachings of Vrulnus, it weighed him down to where his only relief was in his relentless toil.

But he refused to believe Vrulnus was not alive...

Then, early one evening while he was deeply engrossed in a delicate problem in what Vrulnus had called nuclearstatics, *she* came back. He recognized her knock, gentle but firm, patient but persistent.

With a frown, he covered his work and opened the door, and at sight of her the frown evaporated. It didn't have a chance. On the previous occasion the tailor made suit had emphasized cool efficiency. Now, under a light gray coat she wore a taffeta skirt that emphasized a number twenty-four waist and a sheer, white blouse that was but strictly feminine. Unfailingly, her black hair and frank, blue eyes reaffirmed the seeming miracle of her freshness and beauty.

She held out a smooth, unadorned hand and there was nothing to do but to take it in his as she swept into the room.

"I was in the neighborhood and thought I'd see if you were still at the hermitage." Her eyes swept the room, observing much of the same as before—an unmade bed, newspapers on the desk and chair, and dirty dishes in the sink. At sight of the latter, she dimpled at the corners of her delicate mouth, coloring slightly.

He smiled wanly as he released her hand. "I'm not going to be here much longer. My work is nearing completion." Involuntarily, he glanced at the tarpaulin, and her eyes followed his gaze. She studied the mysteriously covered lab bench curiously.

"Ah—Miss Hammer, I can appreciate your professional interest in what may appear to you to be the makings of a sensational news story—my invention, my secrecy and melodramatic seclusion in an old warehouse, and so forth—but I assure you the facts behind all this are quite dull. I am also quite urgently pressed for time and furthermore I still think you should not be running around in this neighborhood alone—particularly at night. You're too attractive a young woman—"

She laughed, showing even white teeth, which accentuated the perfection of her lips. "I didn't know I could penetrate your guard," she said. "You *are* wearing a guard, you know."

"You mean—against women?" In his mind he meant terrestrial women.

She nodded merrily, and the dimples were back. "You're wearing enough armor for a whole Panzer division, and it's quite unnecessary. You see—in one respect I'm an old-fashioned girl. In spite of certain biological susceptibilities of the animal kingdom I am bridging the difference between the sexes with an ordinary, non-biological brand of friendship. Look." She held up both hands. "No notebook, I actually dropped by to find out when you had remembered to eat last."

"Come to think of it, I only had breakfast, but—"

"There. You see? Now I was going to trap you into taking me to dinner, but since you're so busy we can make it hamburgers. There's a stand just three blocks from here."

"Now look here—"

*   *   *

It led to more than hamburgers. There were other visits that he welcomed in spite of his anxieties. Somehow, she lightened his burden. When his mind became stale from the pressure of his calculations and experiments, she regenerated him with her frankness and apparently genuine friendship.

"Of course," he told her one night, "your main objective is the *story* you think lies behind me."

They walked slowly through a dimly lit park near the waterfront. With a characteristic lack of inhibition, she tucked her arm through his.

"For the record," she said, "you're potentially big news. When you tie a woman's intuition in with a reporter's nose, you have a bloodhound that won't quit, Anthony. But aside from all that—the same intuition leads me to believe that you're a very nice person, down underneath all your cloaks and daggers. I *feel* your need for a friend."

"Is this a frustrated mother complex, Lillian?"

"Ungrateful wretch." She laughed, tossing her head so that he caught the perfume of her hair.

Suddenly, Shahn tensed. She felt it and paused, looking up into his face. She saw a man with a look of desperation in his eyes, accompanied by an almost kingly expression of terrible wrath. Looking behind them into the shadows between the trees, he seemed to be ready to strike a deathblow at hidden enemies. She felt the poised, menacing power of him.

"What is it?" she asked, forcing her voice to remain calm.

He turned, pulling her with him as he quickened their pace. "I thought we were being followed."

"Anthony, you wanted me to think your situation was dull and prosaic, I didn't believe you, but—are you really in such danger? I saw the look in your eyes."

"I'm all right. I just want to keep *you* out of all this. Come on."

"I can't keep up with you."

"Sorry."

They reached a streetlight on a corner. Lillian looked back at the shadowy walkway in the park, mystified and not a little frightened.

"Do you really think—"

"I've been expecting it. It may be my overwrought nerves, but for several days now I've had the presentiment that—well—" He looked down at her and smiled, cynically. "That things were—closing in."

"Anthony," she pleaded. "Why can't you share this burden? Can't I be trusted—even now?" Her cool hand pressed his, coaxingly. "You know I can get you help and protection if you want it."

"Let's get off the streets," he answered. "Do you know of a secluded place—close?"

"Only one. Come with me."

They hurried down two short blocks and reached a type of building he had only read about but never entered. The dimly illuminated sign beside the worn concrete steps read: *Saint Anthony Church.*

He watched the Earthwoman closely as she dipped her hand into the holy water and made the sign of the cross. When she led him down the dim aisle between the empty pews and kneeled, he looked up at the candle-lit altar and took in the poignant beauty of dying roses and lilies, the beatific expressions of the Christ and Virgin Mary.

So this was where they practiced their mysterious faith in an extended life beyond the flesh. On Nrlan it was different.

He followed her into the pew and kneeled beside her, looking back at the church door as he did so.

"The church of your patron saint," she whispered. Then she crossed herself and bowed her head, while he looked again at the altar.

On Nrlan, only Ao was eternal. And what was Ao? He wished he knew. Here before him was the apparent basis for certain enduring qualities of the terrestrial tribe. They believed in a sort of duality—one part being extended beyond the life span of the mortal body.

What a thing to believe. If that were true, then what was death? A sort of—of metamorphosis!

He shuddered. No. Better oblivion than to be thrust into some nameless existence beyond the grave.

Suddenly, he was aware that the girl was studying his face.

"Are you a Communist?" she asked, abruptly.

He smiled faintly. "If I am—this is a sly trick of yours—bringing me in here."

Her face fell. "I hoped you were not."

"Well—I'm not."

She breathed a sigh of relief. "I knew it," she whispered. "You couldn't be."

"Why not?"

Her brows contracted in puzzlement. "Please don't be patronizing, Anthony. What is your religion?"

"I have none."

Again, her frown of puzzlement, "Atheist?"

"Not deliberately—rather more by circumstance." Shahn squirmed mentally. This whispered discussion in an empty church could trap him into revelations he was not ready to make. "I—ah—I'm a scientist, that's all." He smiled. "Not very conversant with the *mystical* aspects of the universe. To me there is nothing supernatural."

"Including the soul?" she argued.

"Now *that* is the most interesting philosophical concept I have found—" He paused, warily, trying to rephrase his thought. "I mean—it's so paradoxical. You people claim that you believe in this duality, yet you do very little about it."

"I don't understand."

"Well—it's quite simple. A thing is—or it is not. If you have a soul, which in your conception is indestructible, then why fear death? Yet you fear it. If you really lead a dual existence, then why leave such a marvelous subject in the realm of mysticism and alchemy? Bring it up to date as a scientific fact. If it is in actuality an interlocked subnuclear energy-mass field"—

"An interlocked *what*—?" She was staring at him in confused amazement.

He almost bit his lip. "I'm sorry," he said, looking back at the door of the church. "Lillian, perhaps it's all right now to leave."

She saddened. "I take it you do not approve of religion."

"On the contrary," he answered, getting up. *"Blind* faith is an excellent substitute for the facts, until the facts can be comprehended."

She kneeled hastily in the aisle, crossed herself, then hurried outside ahead of him. She paused on the steps to face him as he came out, his dark eyes searching the shadows of the night.

"Anthony," she said, "I don't know whether you are a sincere genius or an intellectual snob." She smiled softly at him. "Yet somehow I'm not sorry I brought you here."

He took her arm, saying nothing. But he thought: Subnuclear mass-energy. It *could* be possible. Interlocked matter—gross matter plus a counter-balancing infra-pattern—a sub-harmonic, or was gross matter a higher harmonic of the lower energy pattern? Vrulnus would know. He taught that matter was energy; energy is vibration. All manifestations of matter are either harmonics or discords. If only—

"Anthony—what are you thinking?"

"I wish I had a soul."

She stopped, her mouth agape, eyes wide. "What a horrible thing to say. Of course you have a soul."

He smiled. "Have I? If I did, do you know what I would do with it?"

"No."

"I'd photograph it."

Her chin set stubbornly. "Anthony Meade, *I* have a soul—and if you're so smart, you have my permission to photograph it to your heart's content."

He guided her along the street toward the warehouse. "It would be an interesting experiment," he remarked.

*   *   *

Shahn tried hard to shut Lillian Hammer out of his life, but always in the depths of subnuclear physics he was confronted with the subtler mechanics of a persistently infectious pair of blue eyes.

"Damn it," he would exclaim. "She is an Earthwoman. I don't care how lonely it is."

And lonely it was, desperately lonely in a world occupied by several billion people.

Something told him that Lillian Hammer was going to be more than a friend. He rejected the thought repeatedly, but it returned relentlessly—and he was glad in spite of all his rationalizations against it.

Even on the night when he completed the *sarniall* he was glad that she had promised to bring him a snack. While he reasoned against her companionship, his need for her would not be denied. Now that his mighty weapon was ready, he could afford a moment of rest *before* challenging the dark citadel of death that lay deeper than the grave.

When the knock came at the door, his steps toward it were actually lightened by eager anticipation.

"Lillian, I couldn't have waited another—"

As the door swung open, his face froze, eyes staring. Reality thundered back upon him with an icy shock. His bright little forbidden awareness of a resurgent taste for personal happiness shattered discordantly like an old piano dropped from a cliff.

"Dalaney!" he shouted.

Dalaney stood there, smiling as sardonically as might be expected, aiming the dark muzzle of a .45 automatic at the central area of his thorax.

CHAPTER FIVE
Catastrophe

LILLIAN HAMMER quickened her steps at the sound of her own echo in the deserted streets. There was a special element of quietness among the looming shapes of the wharf sheds, which seemed to alert her sensitivity to imminent events. Little things—the wild racing of her heart, a constriction of her throat, the tingling of her nerves—all these combined to warn her that some tragedy of major proportion was about to occur.

Earthquake victims had often mentioned this strange presentiment prior to catastrophe. But once the presentiment arrived, the event always followed swiftly. And so she hurried, not knowing if away or toward the nameless thing which was poised in another moment of time to strike.

"So *there* you are, baby…"

She had been so intent upon reaching Anthony Meade's hidden laboratory that she had been unaware of the long, blue Chrysler behind her. It drifted alongside the curb and stopped. The driver, a heavy-set man with a crew haircut, grinned triumphantly and opened the door.

She almost dropped her "take out" supper package. "Oh Wade," she exclaimed. "How did you trail me?"

"Get in, you foolish virgin. This here is Rape Alley— didn't you know? What the hell's a matter with you doin' a stunt like this? Is *this* the neighborhood your big scoop is in?"

Resignedly but relieved, Lillian got in beside her fellow employee from the Star-Express. "Now don't you spoil this, Wade Kennedy. There's more than just *story* involved."

Wade Kennedy looked down at her package. "Must be. You're taking his supper to him. Some bum, I'd say."

"He's a brilliant scientist, and he's in hiding. Now please—"

Wade guided his car slowly down the dimly lighted street. "Where's this heartthrob live, baby? I'd like to meet him," he added with a glint in his eye.

Lillian tightened her lips. "Wade—so help me. I'll not go there at all if you're going to—"

He patted her knee. "Lil, honey, you're talkin' to your old buddy. Remember?"

She brushed his hand away, though she knew he was more like a brother to her than anything else. Big Wade Kennedy, ex-marine sergeant, former heavyweight boxer, distribution foreman for the Star-Express, he had been her devoted slave for three eventful years.

"But this is too important to spoil now, Wade," she pleaded. "It's—it's too delicate and highly charged with potentials. If you come with me, he might close up—"

"Aw, now Lil. I just was worried about you—"

"Wait, Wade. There's the place. Slow down."

"That big, black shed? In *there?* Damn place looks like a prop for one a them TV foreign spy operas." He stopped the car, wonderingly, and automatically pulled out a package of cigarettes.

She placed her hand on his. "Don't take time for that," she pleaded. "I want to go in."

Wade took hold of her hand. It was cold—and it trembled. "Say! What the—"

Lillian leaned her head abruptly against his shoulder, but quickly recovered. "I'm scared, Wade. Something's going to happen. Something tells me to hurry in there to him—yet to stay away. Oh I'm *glad* you're here."

Wade hunched his powerful frame together, looking at the dark warehouse, then back at her. "Say now—maybe this is gonna get real interesting," he remarked, brightening up at the prospect of action. "Now don't you fret, honey. Your old buddy—"

She shook her head. "You don't understand. He's in immediate danger—*now*. I don't know why, but it's of terrible significance—I'm sure of it."

"Well, let's go in and bring him out. Let's get him some police protection, if that's what you think."

"Oh yes, Wade. Help me convince him to come with us. I feel so *sorry* for him struggling in secret desperation against dangers he can't mention—and so alone. He needs help, Wade, and I know he needs it now—tonight!"

"Okay. Okay. So let's go in and get him."

* * *

"Well, Shahn," said Dalaney, coldly, "you've played your hand—and here's where we *all* show our cards, eh? We've missed you, the *Doctor* and I." As he spoke, he moved slowly into the room while Shahn backed away.

Shahn's eyes narrowed in hate and his nostrils flared angrily. "Menlor, I am *Khal*. Put that gun away or prepare for the consequences. I've known all along you're a collaborator, and now I know Lanis is a Metamorph. I'm going to destroy him and his incubation center."

Dalaney raised his brows in mock surprise. "Really now…" Suddenly, his lips thinned out and his eyes glared at Shahn. "Is this what you wrung out of Pearl Gordon before you eliminated her?"

"I did not—"

"Shut up!" He waved the gun, motioning Shahn to get away from the lab bench. Then he moved toward it and lifted the gleaming *sarniall,* tucking it under his arm. "Your life may still be of use to us, but not nearly as much as before you completed *this.* I am prepared to shoot you down if you resist. You will obey me or die quickly."

Shahn's dark eyes glowered. "Menlor—"

"My name is Charles Dalaney."

"Menlor—there are major stress points in time and history, like mighty hinges upon which swing the gates of destiny for the human race. This moment is one of them. Do you think I would actually allow you to leave here with the *sarniall?"* His whole face darkened with a menacing wrath. *"Put it down!"*

Dalaney studied the other without expression. His knuckles whitened as his grip tightened on the automatic.

It was then that Shahn saw a large, powerfully built man with a crew haircut enter the room silently behind Dalaney. The man grinned confidently and winked at Shahn. The latter had no time to warn the unknown Terrestrial what he was up against.

As Wade Kennedy aimed a rabbit punch at Dalaney's neck that might have stopped a Model T, Dalaney moved with invisible swiftness, before the full force of the blow could take effect. As he turned in a blur of movement, Shahn moved also, letting go of his time sense so that his perspective was now purely Nrlanian and all things Earthly were painfully slow by comparison.

Wade Kennedy was an Earthly ox. He hardly moved at all before Dalaney had lifted him and flung him at the lab bench, where he slumped into unconsciousness. Too slowly for Shahn's quickened eye to follow, a hot soldering iron fell among newspapers along with an open can of acetate dope. The papers smoldered, flames puffed into hungry life—but by that time much had already happened elsewhere.

Shahn tackled Dalaney head-on, knocking the automatic out of his hand. In the struggle, Dalaney dropped the *sarniall* on the floor. Though twice as strong and fast as any Terrestrial, he was no match for Shahn, who seemed bent on destroying him with his bare hands.

As Dalaney went down under Shahn's attack, already feeling the steely band of his grip against his throat, he caught sight of the flames rising up under the lab bench.

"Fire," he gurgled.

One distraction was enough, but when Shahn caught sight of Lillian Hammer entering the room and running for the gun on the floor, her beautiful face twisted in fright and alarm, his grip loosened just enough for Dalaney to break free. Shahn lunged for him, only to be met by a kick in the face.

He blacked out momentarily, while pain shot silvery spangles through the dark immensities that had engulfed him. When he regained consciousness, he heard shots. Lillian Hammer stood there near the doorway, firing the automatic point blank at Dalaney. Smoke was rising fast in the room. Lights and shadows danced weirdly in the presence of the growing flames, but in the midst of it all Shahn saw something that made him cry out in mortal anguish.

"*No!*"

Too late did he stagger to his feet to grapple with the bullet-torn man who held in his dying hands the glowing *sarniall,* its terrible forces concentrated upon the girl. Darkness, like a negative living entity, swirled about Lillian Hammer, and she paled, almost dropping the gun. She staggered toward the dark doorway as Shahn picked up Dalaney and literally smashed him against the wall.

As he turned toward the girl, she faced him unseeingly and fired the gun once more, spasmodically. Shahn grimaced, clutching his middle, and fell across Wade Kennedy's prostrate form where it lay perilously close to the now billowing flames.

As he lost consciousness, he saw Lillian, her face drained of the color of life, staggering into the darkness beyond the door...

* * *

The young nurse opened the door of the hospital room, surveying the patient with a mixture of wonderment and suspicion. Men crowded behind her in the corridor, but only one was admitted.

"That's all, gentlemen," she warned them.

"But that's not fair, Miss," protested one reporter. "Who's this guy, anyway?"

The man who had been admitted turned to the nurse, warning her with a look. As she resolutely went out, closing the door, she was heard to say, "He's a specialist..."

Shahn, lying propped up on the bed, surveyed his visitor through listless eyes. A despair deep as damnation had assailed him. The *sarniall* had been designed to attack the negative life forces of Metamorphs—*not* Lillian Hammer.

The stranger bothered him because he said nothing. He only sat down in a chair beside the bed and looked at him. He was a large man who had suffered a disfiguring accident—probably was a war veteran. His face looked as though it had been burned at one time. Very red and vaguely discolored by faint patches of scar tissue. The eyebrows were gone, and the red toupee was obvious. His eyes were penetrating, his jaw powerful, determined.

When Shahn finally concentrated his attention on him, he pulled out a long red wallet from his coat pocket, opened it, and flashed an impressive ID.

"Sam Hubert," he said, succinctly and almost tonelessly. "Special deputy, Military Intelligence." He smiled faintly. "I'm not an officer. The nurse is right. I'm a specialist."

Shahn's eyes narrowed slightly. "A specialist in *what?*"

"Well, for one thing—in keeping your true identity from the Press. That's Government orders."

"What do you mean—my *true* identity?"

"Relax. My specialty is flying saucers. I've followed them from the day they began arriving—radar statistics, actual photographs, even chased them."

Shahn tensed but controlled himself. He forced a derisive smile. "I thought this was a reputable hospital. How did they let you in?"

Unperturbed, the special deputy began to summarize. "You were shot—apparently through the liver—but I've seen X-rays showing your heart in the center of your thorax. You were lucky, incidentally. The bullet missed the heart. Also, the doctors know about your extra eyelids and your unusual endocrine system, and that your navel is artificial. You're extra-terrestrial." He smiled again, with his mouth but not with his eyes. "That's why I'm here. I'm a sort of one-man secret department—the only one allowed to really specialize in the subject. In case I'm wrong, the Airforce disowns me. If I'm right, then they take over. Until I prove my contentions, I'm sort of expendable, you might say."

Shahn's face hardened. "I will not be interfered with," he said, peremptorily. "The Airforce could do nothing. I—"

The visitor held up his hand. "I haven't finished," he said. "The newspapers are after this story and they want some explanations as to what could account for your strange behavior at the fire."

"Fire? I—hardly remember—except the girl—Lillian Hammer."

"That's just it. Only you knew she was still in the warehouse. Mr. Kennedy—the man who tried to help you regained consciousness in time to carry you out of the burning building about the time the police arrived, followed by ambulances and the fire department. Don't you remember what happened then?"

"I—I went in and got Lillian out of there."

"That's right—and that's what the papers are so excited about. Strong men tried to stop you, because no man could live in that searing heat. But—gravely wounded as you were—you moved like a bullet—you fought and threw police and firemen about as though they were children. You dashed into that inferno and came out alive—carrying the girl. Then you really passed out. The doctors point to an extra gland you possess as the possible explanation."

Shahn's eyes widened. "The girl—Lillian? Is she—"

The agent leaned forward intently.

"That's the sixty-four thousand dollar question, Mr. Meade. Very carefully, I want you to answer me: What do *you* think should be Miss Hammer's status now?—living, dead—or *what?*"

Shahn rose up, then winced, clutching his middle. The other was beside him instantly, pressing him gently hack.

"Take it easy…"

Shahn strained to rise, then relaxed—except for his thoughts. "I take it—she's not dead."

"No."

Shahn closed his eyes, unconsciously biting his lower lip. If he dared believe what he *thought* the *sarniall* had wrought in her, he knew she would prefer to be dead.

"Mr. Kennedy said something about a strange weapon. We found the charred remains of an odd assembly after the fire. Did somebody use it on her?"

"Yes. Dalaney—the only weapon of its kind in the universe—and only fired once—at a wonderful Earth girl like—"

"Dalaney, eh? You knew your assailant, then? Was he also—"

"Yes, he was also an extra-terrestrial. Leave me alone. I'm going, to Lillian." Shahn started to get out of bed in spite of his pain.

"Stay where you are," commanded the agent, sternly. "Now you listen to me. You'll get to see the girl. She is alive and conscious—right here in this hospital. But that's a personal equation. My official duties involve you and your kind. But don't get me wrong. I'm here to help you. I want to know your problem, and you'd better tell me about it."

Shahn felt weak. He subsided again, thinking: She's alive and conscious. That, at least, was something.

"I must see her as soon as possible," he said.

"I'll tell her that—tonight, before I leave. You can see her tomorrow, but I want to be there when you do. Just now, you'd better cooperate with me if you want some friendly assistance."

Shahn studied the other carefully. "What do *you* know about flying saucers?" he asked.

A grim smile answered him. "I was inside one of them when—I think it was a force of your enemies surprised me."

Sham's brows arched, "You *what?*"

"It had cracked up. I was just coming out of it when I walked into some kind of heat ray." He pointed at his scarred face. "They left me for dead. I never did see them. They burned the ship to ashes."

Suddenly, Shahn was considering new possibilities. "All right, Sam Hubert. Maybe I *could* use a friend on the terrestrial side—a secret worker like yourself. If you're going to help, you'll have to know what you're up against. Sooner or later the world will know it is being invaded by forces, which both your kind and my kind must destroy. I'll tell you who I really am—"

* * *

It was a sober faced Sam Hubert who went to see Lillian Hammer, but before he reached her room he was joined by big Wade Kennedy of the Star-Express.

"I was hoping to see her again," Wade told him. "And yet I'm scared stiff. Have you seen that *look* in her eyes?"

They found her bed empty. And they followed her trail, through an open window on the ground floor.

But how were they to know she had gone to church at such a time of night?

Lillian Hammer looked up at the altar and crossed herself again. In her eyes was a vague emptiness, yet her mind was keenly alert—in a cold and lonely sort of way.

She had a memory of former grace—the mystical passion of humility, the awareness of subconscious fulfillment before the face of God.

But now—*emptiness.*

She screamed at the altar, then buried her face in her hands, sobbing uncontrollably. The young priest on duty hurried to her side. He placed a gentle hand on her shoulder.

"It's all right," he told her, peacefully. "Whatever misfortune—none is so great that it may not be healed in this House."

Lillian looked up at him, horrified, her face streaked by tears. "No," she cried, getting up. *"No!"*

And she fled incontinently from the one real sanctuary of her kind—because she was beyond its reach. And only one man on Earth could know the answer.

She had to find him, so she retraced her steps once more to the hospital. If *he* could not heal her more than mortal wound, then nothing mattered—neither life nor death. For even suicide would be futile . . .

The little cherubic faced man with the merry blue eyes presented his credentials at the night desk of the hospital. "Doctor Lanis," he said. "You have one of my patients here—Anthony Meade."

The nurse looked up, startled. "One of *your* patients?"

"Yes." Lanis smiled disarmingly, tapping his head. "Mental case," he explained. "He escaped my sanitarium in Los Angeles, and I'm afraid he can be quite violent. However, I am prepared to take him back with me."

"I'm afraid he can't be released without proper authorization."

"Oh I think he can."

And Lanis was right, because his kind had a way with people—like possessing one's mind and will and making a person think everything was quite as it should be.

*   *   *

Shahn was heard to cry out in terrible alarm when Lanis was admitted to his room—but then such "mental cases" always did resist recapture. Did not the kind little doctor say his patient could be violent?

A smiling, glazy-eyed hospital staff even helped Lanis get Shahn's straightjacketed body into the black sedan that was waiting to take him away.

While Sam Hubert and Wade Kennedy searched the night for Lillian Hammer.

And while Lillian walked alone in the streets toward the hospital—bent on finding Shahn.

CHAPTER SIX
Revelation

THE WINDOW of the hospital room was locked. She moved along the dark wall of the building, behind the shrubbery, searching for other windows. All were locked against her, as though now she was no longer a part of the world she had known. In the dim illumination of the distant parking lot, the upper story windows were like the eyes of an alien jury, looking sternly down.

Animal! A humanoid freak, devoid of the eternal *essence*—a mere organism of flesh and blood and nerve ganglia—barred forever from the promise of extension beyond the grave.

She bit at her knuckles, heedless of the pain. Anthony Meade had built the instrument, which had given her this negative existence. Only he would know the answer to her plight, if any answer were available in Heaven, Earth or Hell. Well—why not go in the front entrance? She was not a prisoner. She would demand to see Anthony Meade—tonight, *now.*

She hesitated at the driveway. Before the entrance was a long, black sedan. Several attendants in white coats were struggling with a squirming figure in a straightjacket, under the supervision of a small, professional looking man with a black goatee.

Suddenly, her heart seemed to pause when the man in the straightjacket cried out and she recognized his voice.

"You can hypnotize *them,* Lanis, but not the *Khal.* You'd better kill me now. If I get loose you won't have another chance—"

The little main interrupted sharply with a word in a foreign tongue. He signaled to his chauffeur, who opened the rear door of the sedan and helped the attendants to deposit the victim's body on the back seat.

Lillian clenched her small fists, her thoughts racing wildly. Another enemy had struck at Anthony Meade—a more bizarre enemy than her wildest imaginings had included. A master hypnotist!

And they were taking him away somewhere. If she let him get out of her sight—if they harmed him—she might never have a chance, herself. If any antidote existed, only they would know.

Without allowing the hovering phantom of fear to deter her in her wild purpose, she darted unseen to the opposite rear door of the sedan. The chauffeur and the weird man with the goatee were momentarily engaged in herding the hospital staff back inside the building.

"Lillian," hissed Shahn, as he saw her crawl in on the floor of the car and quietly close the door behind her. "In the name of Eternity, save yourself. Get out."

"In the name of Eternity," she whispered back, "I am here. Be still."

* * *

Sam Hubert's scar-lined face was grimly set under the burden of premonition when he entered the hospital lobby followed by a bewildered and worried Wade Kennedy.

"What's going on in here?" he demanded to know, as he addressed the night receptionist.

"Oh, Mr. Hubert, we've called the police," exclaimed the nurse. "But you're *just* the man we're looking for."

Swiftly and with admirable coherence in spite of her fright, the woman related what had happened, aided meanwhile by all the other nurses and interns who had been victimized by Lanis.

"It wasn't exactly hypnotism," explained one student doctor. "It was rather—a direct dominance of the will. We knew we were being coerced but we couldn't do a thing about it."

"Yeah," put in another. "It was like in a dream—a nightmare. That guy's too weird to be running around loose."

"Well, he's captured an *extremely* important man," Hubert told them. "Did you get the stranger's name?"

"Oh yes," cried the nurse at the desk. "Doctor Lanis. That was it."

"Hmm. Lanis and Dalaney. Dalaney got killed trying to capture Meade. Now Lanis takes him. Which way did he go?"

"He said something about a sanitarium in Los Angeles."

"Sanitarium, eh? *That* may be a gross understatement."

There was more. Before the police arrived, one intern hurried downstairs from one of the patient's rooms. Someone had seen the figure of a woman enter the sedan from the shrubbery.

"Hey," Wade exclaimed. "That must've been Lillian."

"Probably," commented Hubert, somberly. He paused, listening. In the distance he could hear police sirens approaching. He started out the front door, with Wade at his heels.

He ran like a man with an artificial leg, but he ran swiftly, and Wade had all he could do to keep up with him in spite of years of roadwork as a fighter. It was only when they had reached Hubert's custom made sports car in the parking lot that the latter realized Wade was behind him.

"Sorry," he said, getting inside quickly. "This is a solo flight."

Wade got in and slammed the door. "That's what you think, buddy, Lillian Hammer is a particular friend of mine. Get going!"

Hubert glared at him peremptorily, then relaxed slightly. "Wade, I'm even ducking the police because they'd only be in the way. I'm the only man in Military Intelligence knows enough about this thing to even guess what to do. I've run into this thing before. Look at my face. My leg is artificial, too. That was from a light skirmish with them the last time. This time I *think* I'm prepared. You, most certainly, are not—and never will be. Your chances of living through it are about one in a thousand."

Wade glared back. "You're wasting time. How about trying highway 101 and keeping our eyes peeled for a long, black sedan?"

"That's what I had in mind. But get this. So much is involved here that if you deter my efforts you will have to become expendable. I like you, so I should kick you out."

"Are you gonna drive this heap—or am I?"

Hubert gave Wade one more peremptory glare, but there was a grim light of appreciation in his narrowed eyes as he started the car and roared abruptly out of the hospital grounds. He drove unhesitatingly through a red signal, swerving screeching around a hay truck with effortless ease. In a matter of seconds, the speedometer soared to seventy, then to eighty. Wade resisted the impulse to put his feet through the floorboards. He gritted his teeth.

"I've been waiting a long time for Meade's enemies to show their hand," Hubert said, evenly. "This is it."

"I sure wished to hell I knew what this is all about," grumbled Wade. "Especially what's wrong with Lillian. Back in that warehouse fire I didn't see everything that went on— but *you* found out. What happened to her?"

"She may not know—*yet*. But I have an idea that's why she went with Meade in that car. She doesn't dare let him out of her sight. She thinks he's the only living being with an answer to her predicament."

"Do you think she's right?"

Sam Hubert maneuvered the car with masterful skill between two lanes of opposed traffic. Headlights glared, horns wailed mournfully, tires screeched—but on he went, never diminishing his speed, watching the road ahead for the long, black sedan.

"There is only one who might help her now," he said, finally. "And it isn't Anthony Meade."

* * *

The long, black sedan purred smoothly and swiftly along the highway. From her position on the floor of the car, Lillian could not see the doctor and his chauffeur in the front seat. All she was aware of was Shahn and the fastenings of his straightjacket, which she struggled to untie.

He lay there silently watching her, or at times his dark eyes would look up at the driver. Finally, when she had actually unfastened the jacket and he was free to move, he pulled her face next to his and whispered. They were passing a heavy line of trucks and it was unlikely he could have been heard in the front seat.

"Now get down and hang on," he told her.

Their faces had never been this close before. Their eyes, wide with their mutual anxiety, intimate in the proximity of the unknown, were only inches apart.

"Are you all right?" he added.

"You're wounded," she whispered back, as she saw him wince. Her hand touched his in the dark.

"Watch it," he warned her, looking up ahead.

As she turned involuntarily to look at the front seat, she gasped, then covered her mouth. They had started out with two men in the front, but now there was only *one*. The chauffeur was still at the wheel, but the strange little man with the goatee had disappeared.

"Down," hissed Shahn.

As Lillian ducked down, trembling in nameless fear, Shahn spoke to the driver in a strange tongue that she could not associate with any language she had ever heard before.

"The language of the *Khals* is dead," answered the chauffeur, in English, without looking back. "And so is the race. Resign yourself, Shahn. We belong to the mutation. It is inevitable."

Gaping in wonderment, Lillian searched the tense face of her companion. Once again she saw there that strange kingly expression of wrath as he stared back at the chauffeur.

"There is yet time," he insisted. "Your strength is in me— if you will serve me—*all* of you."

"Silence—or *he* will return," warned the driver.

"Pah! It is a great effort for *them* to extend themselves to so far from their chrysalides."

"You do not know their great power. Now be still."

Shahn concentrated every faculty of his mind on the other man. He placed in his mind a vision of a tree falling suddenly across the road.

The car swerved, skidded, jumped the shoulder and crashed through a fence, turning over just as Lillian screamed. The chauffeur struck his head against the windshield and went limp over the wheel.

Lillian did not see the next thing happen, but in another instant she was outside the car, rolling over the ground in Anthony Meade's arms. Then they were crawling under bushes, and finally he bade her lie still, while he looked back.

The sedan lay on its side in a gulley ten feet below the highway. Up above, cars were skidding to a halt. There was a sound of people shouting.

"Come on," he exclaimed, pulling her to her feet. "Run!"

Strangely, he was leading her away from the highway into a clump of trees.

"Why this way?" she gasped. "The people are stopping. We can get help."

"No! They'll attract attention to us. Do as I say. If *he* comes back, they can't help."

"But—where did he go—? the *little* man—?"

"Never mind. Just hurry."

After half an hour of wandering through back woods and meadows, they found a combination tool shed and pump house near an irrigation canal. Inside the crude wooden building was a single bunk and several old blankets. Shahn took her to the bunk and they both sat down, breathing hard from their exertions. He held his abdomen, trying to still the pain that was there.

"Lie down here," she told him, and he did.

"I feel weak," he said, looking up at her, "but I'm all right. It's just the pain—no bleeding."

They were both silent a while, looking at each other. Suddenly, however, she burst into tears. "Tell me what this is all about," she cried out. "Who *are* you? What is it your enemies want? And what has *happened* to me? I feel that my soul is *dead.*"

She sobbed bitterly as he reached out to her, and then she was lying beside him, her body shaking momentarily in her grief and nameless fear.

"Such a curse as this is beyond the curse of Hell," she almost screamed. "You have to help me or I'll go mad. I can't stand it. I'm dead, but I'm alive—for what? Oh Anthony—! Anthony *Please*—for the love of God help me."

His heart went out to her there in the dark that was laden with dread beyond her own imaginings, for they were not yet safe. He knew, even as he listened with the unearthly auditory senses of his kind to the night and the brooding sky.

Suddenly he held her to him, pressing her face tightly against his, holding her head and her body still. "Life is not ended," he told her. "Get hold of yourself, Lillian."

"Myself is gone," she wailed. "I am nothing but an empty shell of flesh."

"And so am I—and all of my kind."

Then Lillian was still. Her quivering ceased. She lay there close pressed against him, absorbing the implication of his words. Finally, she pulled slowly away and sat up, looking at him without expression, her face stained with tears.

"What did you say?"

He tried to smile but couldn't. "Your kind has been raised in the concept of duality," he told her. "It is hard for you to conceive of a people without souls, as you call them. Perhaps, long ago in our past—"

Her eyes widened. "Anthony! Are you insane?"

"No, but I am not of your world. And my name is not Anthony. It is Shahn. I was born on another planet, Lillian. I am extra-terrestrial. That should explain a lot of things to you—my strange seclusion, the high-voltage battery, the language you heard me speak, the strange weapon in the warehouse—the mystery of Doctor Lanis—and that night in the church..."

Lillian did not get up. She sat rigidly on the edge of the bunk, suddenly separated from him as though by an invisible gulf that was as measureless as time and space. Her first reaction had been one of utter disbelief. But then she remembered the church. Not even an atheist would have acted so strangely. Once she allowed the seed of credulity to be planted, it grew in fertile ground.

"It—it's difficult—to grasp," she said, tonelessly.

"Of course." He groped for her hand and held it gently but firmly. "Fiction is flirtation. The unknown revealed is like sin, because it assails the citadels of thought, knowledge and tradition. As to the virgin the awesome experience of reality engenders the instinct of preservation, so the cloistered egotism of a world-biased mentality must quail before the baleful eye of cosmic revelation. Here am I—a human being from realms beyond the sky. But—granted this, you had not imagined I could exist without a soul. Just as it is shocking and strange to you, so was it a mind-staggering concept to me that such a thing as duality could be. It is marvelous, and it begins to explain many things—many things—"

Lillian remained speechless, feeling alone, lost, chilled by the etheric winds of void without end—herself a microbe of life, the world a grain of sand—the stars more remote than the dawn of light. Her mind reeled in vertigo.

The man beside her began to talk. He knew that when the foundations of reason are shaken a new foundation must be filled in quickly. He told her of Nrlan, his own beloved world now long dead and shattered. He told her of the Metamorphs, and of Vrulnus—and Rospor—of the black chrysalides that lay in the contaminated soil of Earth, from which the evil extensions of the Metamorphs emanated, assuming human form or any other form they chose—of how they already dominated the world, its governments, posing as well known chosen leaders in every important position of authority.

He described the plight of the Nrlani and how they were scattered over the Earth, eking out their temporary existence against the time of mandatory suicide, to avoid the mutation, and of how the Metamorphs sought them out for the purpose of perpetuating their own kind.

He told her of his own purpose and his desperate hope—and of their danger, even now.

"If I built one *sarniall*, I can build another, and they know it. If I were to give my own kind even a single sign of hope, I would be hailed as the *Khal*, and my strength would grow. They can't afford to let me get out of their hands. I tried to warn you, Lillian, but I was weak. I should have turned you away the first day you saw me, but I couldn't."

She looked down at him, while she pushed away her tears with the heel of her hand. "Why not?"

Again, he tried a smile that failed. "Why burden you now?"

But she guessed the reason. "I was strangely attracted to you, too, Shahn," she said. "I am as much to blame."

He emitted a dry, bitter laugh. "Two people who are perfectly matched often never meet, but we who are twice separated from one another by insurmountable barriers—" He waved his hand, unable to go on.

"There is much we have in common now," she answered. "We are thrown together in our mutual misfortune. Where else can I go but with you? If you die, I am without reprieve. If you live, you may still find a solution—or this great man, Vrulnus. You or he must solve it. Without that single shred of hope, even my mind will die."

"Then—the very magnitude of the barrier between us is the bond that holds us together. Lillian, as I owe my people the chance to live again—I also owe it to you."

Their mutual situation engendered a poignant loneliness that must be shared as the only defense against itself. Together, they were a finite island suspended above the reasonless abyss. Apart—mere atoms in chaos.

They clung to each other suddenly like children on a raft in a flood. Rationalizations were beyond the sphere of their emotions. At length, they slept lightly, and the night deepened in its silence and its intimate darkness.

CHAPTER SEVEN
The Debut of Arms

"THERE," shouted Wade, pointing ahead at the traffic jam. "I see a sedan in the ditch."

"Looks like it," said Hubert, slamming on the brakes to avoid a Highway Patrol car as it made a U-turn with red lights ablaze.

When the sports car had skidded around twice and come in on the shoulder backwards, Sam Hubert jerked on the emergency, and both of them were out, running toward the wreck.

"Who the hell are *you?*" shouted the Highway Patrol officer, angrily, already waiting for them on the bank.

Sam flashed his credentials. "This is a G-2 item," he said swiftly, climbing down toward the car. Stand by. I'll want your radio."

Grimly obedient, the officer followed, and the three of them inspected the sedan. Even the chauffeur had disappeared.

"There's an APB out," said the officer. "Look for a black sedan and a Doctor Lanis—captured a man wanted by G-2. They're gone, so what's next?"

Hubert straightened up from the wreck and looked off into the wilderness. "You'll need a posse to search that area," he answered.

"You think Doctor Lanis is out there?"

"No—but perhaps his chauffeur—and Anthony Meade."

"And Lillian Hammer," put in Wade.

"Lillian Hammer—who's she?"

Hubert looked up at the sky. "I'd better use your radio," he said, irrelevantly. "Where's your car, officer?"

As they reached the shoulder, curious bystanders crowded in.

"Anybody hurt, officer?"

"Betcha they were drunk, eh?"

The officer waved them off. "You people move on," he told them. "You're blocking the highway."

Wade Kennedy looked wistfully off into the wilderness, wondering about Lillian. He heard Hubert at the radio in the patrol car, asking to be connected through a police phone-patch with somebody in S.A.C. Suddenly, Hubert was raising his voice.

"I don't give a damn *what* your regulations are," he shouted. "I want General Morrison!"

Wade and the officer exchanged glances, wryly. When the general was finally connected, Sam Hubert said something in a low tone that was unintelligible to both men, prefacing his remarks with a code reference. Then—abruptly he signed off and got out of the car.

"You can call your posse now," he said to the officer. "We'll wait in my car."

"Whaddayou mean *wait?*" argued Wade. "Aren't we gonna look for Lillian?"

Hubert motioned him along as he hurried back to the sports car. "Somebody else may be looking for her and Meade," he said. "That's what we have to watch for. Come on."

When they got in the car, Hubert started up the engine. "Look for a road or a cow path. We'll drive into the area."

"I like action," said Wade, "but I sure hate mysteries."

"You invited yourself into this one. Now shut up and watch the sky."

"What for?"

"Flying saucers."

"*What?*"

"That's what I was talking to General Morrison about. I asked him for a fighter plane cover—because if they ever show up they'll show up now. They can't afford to let Meade escape—and that isn't his real name anyway." He rounded a narrow dirt road and jerked the car into it, traveling rapidly.

"Say, what the hell is this? I think you're going nuts."

"I told you you weren't equipped for what's involved," snapped Hubert. "Just don't make yourself a nuisance."

"But—flying saucers! For Christ's sake—all I want is Lillian!"

"Won't do you any good if *they* show up. I'm trying to ward them off from here."

Hubert found a small hillock under a tree and scared off a lowing herd of cattle. He parked the car.

"This is a good spot," he said. "Keep your eyes open."

Wade swore. He started to get out. Hubert took hold of him.

"Stay here," he said.

Wade swung his hand, knocking the other's arm away. "You like your health, you leave me alone, sonny. I'm gonna look—"

It was all he had a chance to say. Hubert was out of the car after him like a cat. Wade swung at him swiftly, but he hardly knew what happened after that. He woke up a moment later, back in the car, with Sam Hubert glaring at him, a steel-like grip holding him down.

"So you're going to be a hero," Sam snarled through his teeth, "and run into the danger zone after your girl friend—holding her in one arm while you flight off the weapons of another world with your free hand? Look at my face! Do you want Lillian Hammer to get what I got? Now shut up and do as I say or I'll throttle you—right here and now."

Wade studied his captor for half a minute without expression. Then he grinned. "You have a way with you, chum. But I read you good—even if it's still crazy."

Hubert let him sit up. "We'll just wait," he said.

Wade straightened his tie, brushed back his hair, and ruefully rubbed a bruised chin. "Be kinda tough on that posse you're sending in here," he commented. "You didn't warn *them* about flying saucers."

"That officer would have become a bottle-neck like you if I'd told him the truth, but his men may arrive in time to be witnesses to what I suspect. That's all I want—witnesses..."

"To what—flying saucers?"

"Yes."

"Well, even if I could swallow this baloney about flying saucers—it still wouldn't make sense. How are mere jet fighters gonna take on *those* things. Why not use Nukes?"

"These are not jets. You may see a new kind of plane in action. Do you know anything about science?"

"High school physics is all—plus what I read in the comics."

"Ever heard about why certain gases like nitrogen are inert?"

"I flunked out on that part but had to make it up to play football, so it's one thing I still remember. Something about their atomic structure, I guess. The outer electron shell—"

"Exactly. Now suppose a certain type of intense radiation could change the outer shell of the nitrogen atom."

"It might have a valence—maybe combine—hey—!"

"That's it. Combine with oxygen. Combustion of the air, itself. These new fighters have radiation engines. They run on air. In upper altitudes their velocity is drastically unlimited."

"Yeow! Who invented that?"

"It's a little item I gave the Airforce, myself."

"*You?*"

"Don't get excited. I didn't invent it. It was a little piece of science I borrowed before I got burned for my efforts."

"You mean—that's how flying saucers operate?"

"Not entirely, but it's a principle they sometimes use in the atmosphere when magnetic disturbances are too great."

"How did you find out all this?"

"We've talked enough. Let's watch."

Wade had no recourse but to sit there with Sam Hubert and watch the dark, silent sky. He fumed, unbelieving helpless, yet not without hope.

* * *

Shahn opened his eyes to find his lips brushing Lillian's soft cheek. She was asleep in his arms. His heart ached for her, but she was not the cause of his sudden alertness.

A sound, which would have been inaudible to terrestrial ears, stirred his instincts alive. Far away and faint, yet insistently close as the air he breathed—like a static condition. In fact, it *was* a static condition. As his lips brushed Lillian's dark hair, a slight spark jumped at him.

He sat up, and she opened her eyes. "Shahn, what is it?"

For answer, he pulled her to him, holding her close. "Just sit tight love. We have no other choice."

"Shahn. You trembled. You know what it is. Something's coming after us…"

"Yes, but if we just stay where we are—"

"But what *is* it, Shahn?"

"You might as well know. I told you I was important to them. They're searching for me up there right now."

"You mean—aircraft?"

"In a flying saucer—as you call them. They're really interstellar space ships."

She held herself tightly to him. "On Shahn—I can't grasp it all. Are you sure? I can't hear a thing."

"What do you feel?"

"You."

"Brush your hand through my hair."

She did so and it crackled like cat's fur.

"Magnetics," he said. "It charges the air when they're close." He felt her tremble and he held her to him. "If they find us—stay close. Maybe I can buy my way out of it—and you in the bargain."

"Is there nothing we can do?"

"Nothing—not now. They can detect our infra-red. You know your science."

The sound deepened until it became audible in Lillian's ears. It throbbed in the air around them. Suddenly, a bluish light flooded the landscape outside, and Lillian screamed.

In the same instant, the figure of a man appeared in the doorway of the shack, limned weirdly in the bluish light.

"Come out, Shahn," the man said. "They are here." It was Lanis' chauffeur.

Shahn sprang from the bunk and was at the man's throat before Lillian realized they were not alone. But he forgot that he was weak and wounded. The other was stronger and quicker than he was now.

Lillian saw the stranger trip Shahn, saw the two fall on the ground together. The air throbbed with a crescendoing warning of doom as she searched frantically for something to use as a weapon. Her hand suddenly closed on the handle of a steel pick.

In that moment, two more men appeared at the door. One of them moved almost as swiftly as Shahn, throwing himself into the fight. The other lunged toward her. She raised the pick instinctively, ready to kill.

"*Lillian!*"

The swirling blue light suddenly illumined the homely, square-jawed face of Wade Kennedy. One big fist caught the descending pick. Behind him, Lillian saw the chauffeur break loose from his new opponent. He was blinded, his eyes gouged, but a pistol glinted in his hand as Sam Hubert froze, facing him.

"Wade!" Lillian screamed, pointing.

Wade turned, saw and struck with a long-armed, professional lunge, and the steel pick buried itself in the center of the chauffeur's startled, frozen face.

Nausea welled up within her, but she fought it. She kneeled beside Shahn, who was on his hands and knees shaking his head.

"Listen to me," exclaimed Sam Hubert. "We can't run for it. It's too late. We'll be captured—all of us. But don't show resistance. Play for time—get it? You *must* play for time."

Shahn staggered to his feet. "What do you know about it, Hubert?" he asked bitterly. "I'll give the instructions here. You stay out of this. It's me they want—and I know what to bargain with."

"But you don't represent the government of the United States. I do. Just do as I say and no heroics."

"I won't argue the point. It's *my* kind we're dealing with—and I am *Khal.*"

"You are if Vrulnus is dead."

"I told you he was."

"Well—chins up, everybody. Here they come."

Shahn looked curiously at Wade Kennedy, who had his arm around Lillian. *Everybody* seemed to want to take over around here. The old wrath of the *Khals* rose within him. He stepped proudly to the doorway then and faced his captors, eyes blazing, his nostrils distended, lips tight-pressed together.

The flat space ship lay in the meadow before them, its observation dome ports aglow. Half a hundred Nrlanians stood outside the shack waiting for him. In their hands were sonic heaters.

"Holy tomcats," muttered Wade. "I'd feel saner if I was dreaming…"

"Put your weapons away," Shahn commanded, addressing the Nrlanians in their own tongue. "You would not use them because you still need a *Khal.* If Vrulnus is gone, then I am your only hope. Be with me and you can fight to victory—or die without shame. Serve the Metamorphs and you deny yourselves the last reality of honor as men."

The fifty Nrlanians observed him in apathetic silence, but Wade stared at him in stunned amazement.

"Serve yourselves and call me *Khal*—or I will show you how to die," he shouted.

"Ye gods," ejaculated Wade, hoarsely. "Meade is one of *them.*"

"Be quiet," whispered Lillian. "Control yourself, Wade, please."

"But it ain't easy. Whaddayou expect? This isn't Market Street at high noon, baby. This is the D.T.'s at midnight! Brother. You were *really* working on a scoop, honey."

Sam Hubert placed a restraining hand on Shahn's arm. "Remember," he said, "the girl. If you resist now we all die. I told you to play for time. I have a reason Shahn."

"Hey," exclaimed Wade, insuppressibly. "What about those planes? The General musta stood you up, Hubert."

Shahn turned upon Hubert, his teeth flashing in anger. "Don't give *me* your airforces and terrestrial defenses—they're a waste of time here. I alone can evaluate—"

Sam Hubert produced a small automatic. "I'll give you this," he whispered tensely. "You don't know as much as you think you do. These are not ordinary Nrlanians—they are a new breed created by the Metamorphs and your words could not have the slightest effect on them. You must surrender to them—*now.*"

Wade and Lillian opened their eyes wide, looking from Sam Hubert to Shahn and back again.

"*You,*" exclaimed Shahn. "You're—Nrlanian—a collaborator…"

"Why the dirty—" Wade started to exclaim.

Sam Hubert stepped out of range of both men's fists. Though with a slight limp, he moved swiftly, backing toward the Nrlanian force from the ship, his automatic trained on Shahn.

"Surrender to them, Shahn or die futilely—and your friends with you."

Shahn turned to his two terrestrial companions, but principally to Lillian. "All right," he muttered in a low tone. "He *said* play for time, didn't he? I'll play for time, all right. Come on."

CHAPTER EIGHT
Main Base

SILENTLY, the strange Nrlanian crew surrounded the little group, including Sam Hubert. They disarmed the latter and herded them all toward the waiting ship.

"I'm not a collaborator—nor am I Nrlanian," Hubert whispered to Shahn. "You will simply have to trust me—"

Shahn turned his head slowly, surveying the other through narrowed eyes. "Then how do you know so much?"

"Yeah, how come?" put in Wade. "And why'd you want Meade to surrender so bad?"

Hubert smiled wryly, his eyes scanning the sky quickly. "I told you I was a specialist, Shahn."

"Shahn?" Wade frowned in puzzlement. "But I thought—"

"Wade, hush," admonished Lillian anxiously.

"Silence," commanded a Nrlanian officer. "Move along quickly."

Shahn detected a sudden, high-pitched wail from the ship, which was far above the audibility range of Terrestrials. He looked at Wade and Lillian and saw that they were unaware of it. He looked at Sam Hubert, whose face remained expressionless.

"They're receiving an alarm signal," he told them. "Perhaps your Airforce is approaching."

There was no opportunity for private comment, as they were forced to climb a steep ramp and enter the ship, yet Wade Kennedy could not repress his reaction to the other world craft.

"Holy Toledo! This is real crazy—a flying hallucination…"

The spacecraft had one main deck, circular, with a control chamber in its center and an observation dome on top. Whatever fuel or machinery there was to propel it lay unrevealed beneath their feet.

There were a number of hiberbunks on the deck, and toward these the Nrlanians led Lillian, Wade, and Sam Hubert. Shahn stood among his captors and watched Hubert closely.

"Say! What *is* this?" complained Wade. "They gonna strap us down for the kill?"

"You had better get yourselves strapped onto those bunks," advised Shahn. "Our time sense is different than yours. What is a slow bank turn to us is a high gravity pullout to you. The bunks will help."

As a Nrlanian officer directed Lillian to lie down on the bunk, she looked back at Shahn, questioningly. "Shahn—?"

"It's your only chance of survival," he told her. "I'll try to get them to take it as easy as possible."

Wade strained his big muscles just once while in the grip of two Nrlanians, but he found their grip unyielding.

"He's right, Lil," he told the girl. "This is like fighting dinosaurs with a sling-shot. We better get strapped in pronto."

As the two got onto the bunks and the Nrlanians began to strap them down, Shahn's eyes met Sam Hubert's. The latter hesitated a moment beside one of the bunks, then shrugged and lay down on it.

"Are you sure that's necessary—for you?" asked Shahn.

"Not taking any chances," Hubert replied, as he was strapped in.

"Evidently."

AS THE SHIP finally leapt upward, the muffled shriek of a passing aircraft was heard outside.

"Hey," cried Wade, though the blood had drained from his face under the pressure of acceleration. "Uncle Sam showed up, after all, Hubert."

"They won't fire on us now," replied Sam, laboriously. "They must assume terrestrial captives may be on board—but they'll follow us to see where we land."

"Can they keep up with us?"

"I'm certain of it."

"Wow…"

The deck of the ship blurred before Wade's eyes as it careened wildly and shot off in a new direction. Shahn strained in the hands of his captors, watching Lillian. She had fainted.

"Consider their lives," he demanded. "I'll cooperate if you take it easy."

"You'll cooperate," smiled one of the officers coldly, "when you see what we have to show you…"

There was no further sign that they were being followed by the new type Airforce jets. In a matter of a few minutes, the ship began to descend. It paused, hovering for a moment, as though waiting for a signal, and then suddenly dropped so abruptly that Shahn and the other Nrlanians were momentarily suspended above the deck.

When they pulled up for a landing, the passengers lying on the bunks, apparently including Sam Hubert, blacked out entirely. Shahn watched Lillian tensely but relaxed when he finally saw her turn her head and open her eyes to look at him.

He tried to smile reassuringly, but his thoughts were racing. This ship had probably arrived in one of the hiding places of Metamorph power on Earth. This is what he had been looking for. But what purpose had his captors in preserving the lives of the others?

There was no time left to conjecture. The prisoners on the bunks were promptly unstrapped, and the four of them were herded down the ramp and out of the ship.

Their first reaction to their surroundings was a studious silence as they gazed about them with a mixture of awe, incredulity, suspicion and alarm, each according to his own temperament. They had entered a mountain and now found themselves in a large subterranean chamber that housed fully ten of the interstellar craft, and which Sam Hubert in particular examined with an almost desperate concentration. A smoothly excavated tunnel gave access to other departments of the underground establishment.

"This place looks like it's been here for years," observed Wade. "Some engineering, I'd say, to carve all this out and hide all the dirt without us Earthmen knowing a thing about it."

"On our own planet," Shahn explained, "our environment required of us, at times, a semi-subterranean existence due to excessive temperatures on the surface, or excessive cold. We learned to develop very efficient means of burrowing, as we were a hibernating race." His eyes met Lillian's, but he saw reflected there no reaction to this further revelation of their differences—only a loyal understanding—and his heart went out to her. "You see, there was no dirt to conceal here. We use disintegrators."

"Disintig—yipes! And I thought that's what kids got for sending in box tops. Say, how long have you antmen been around here, anyway?"

"Wade! Don't be unkind," admonished Lillian. "Shahn is not our enemy. He is equivalent to a Prime Minister or emperor in exile."

"I should say about thirty years since the first ships landed," Shahn answered him.

"Well, if you're on our side," persisted Wade, "what I'd like to know is what it's all about. What do your people really want—why are they hiding—and what are you trying to stop them from doing?"

The Nrlanians had been waiting for a ground vehicle, which now drew up before them, and the prisoners were directed to enter it.

"It's a long story, Wade," said Shahn. "But you may have a demonstration of what I have fought against before we're through."

The ground vehicle was more like a flat-bottomed excursion boat with a "domeliner" top as Wade described it. In spite of a load of twenty passengers, it floated lightly off the ground and darted unerringly into the tunnel shaft.

"Brother," exclaimed Wade hanging on to the seat in front of him. "Coney Island was never like this. How does it work?"

"You Terrestrials overlooked a great deal in magnetics," Shahn explained. "We are riding a magnetic wave much as you would ride a surfboard."

There was not much conversation for a while, as all eyes searched ahead for signs of their destination. But at times Lillian studied Shahn's face, absorbing from him the mounting tensions she knew he felt. Yet, surprisingly, she was without fear in his presence, in spite of the dark, unholy power that seemed to control their mutual destiny now. Again her instincts came to the fore, impressing upon her the conviction that this tall, proud, dark-eyed man would assert his kingly qualities and ultimately provide her with a happy solution to her untenable nightmare.

But the test of that—and the crisis of their lives—lay immediately ahead in the lair of the Metamorphs...

They arrived in a subterranean terminal and were led promptly away through an adjoining passageway into wider avenues, where hundreds of Nrlanians were in evidence.

"Hubert," said Shahn, as they walked along between their captors, "you mentioned that this was a new breed of Nrlanians. I can see that something is different about them—but what is it?"

The Intelligence agent had altered strangely since entering the Nrlanian stronghold. He was wary, silent, broodingly preoccupied, his narrowed eyes darting everywhere, taking in every detail of his surroundings.

"Brainwashing is a good name for what ails them," he commented, crisply. "They are like drones. Their will belongs to the Metamorphs. They are also the result of accelerated incubation. They are called *drals*."

"Where did you learn all this?"

"I told you I was a sp—"

In that moment, Lillian gasped. She put her hands out in front of her, gropingly, as though blinded. Wade Kennedy collided with a guard who had stopped in front of him, and Sam Hubert came to an abrupt halt. His eyes seemed to search about him without focusing upon anything, like a man who found himself in total darkness.

"Hey! The lights went out," yelled Wade.

Shahn squinted at the ceiling. There were two tubes running the length of each passage. One, he could observe, was now dark, while the other glowed only with the Jansi light—visible to Nrlanians only. As far as Earthborn humans were concerned, the tunnel was in total darkness.

The guards were observing Sam Hubert—as was Shahn. Suddenly, one of the guards raised the butt of his sonic heater and brought it down swiftly toward Sam Hubert's head, just grazing it, but not quite touching him. The latter did not flinch, nor did he seem to see the guard in front of him.

Just as abruptly, the regular light returned to the tunnel and the march was resumed without explanation.

"Thought for a minute somebody forgot to pay the light bill," commented Wade, wryly. "Boy! When it gets dark down here you can *feel* it."

"I wonder what *that* was all about?" commented Hubert, to Shahn.

"You know so much—you should understand what happened, Sam."

"But I don't."

"Well—they just proved you're a Terrestrial."

"How?"

"I'll explain later. It looks like we're arriving."

They came to a halt before a gate that Wade described as a "disc-valve." The ponderous metal disc slid back into a niche in the wall as they approached—and six Nrlanian guards in dark blue uniforms met them.

"These are not *drals,*" said Sam, quickly. "They're regular Nrlanians."

Shahn glared at them haughtily, and they stared curiously back at the man who on their own world might have become *Khal.* The *drals* halted, and it appeared that they were not permitted beyond the gate.

"Come with us," commanded one of the new guards.

As they marched onward, Shahn questioned them in peremptory tones, "How many are there of you who choose allegiance to the Metamorphs rather than to your *Khal?*"

"Your questions, Shahn," replied the first Nrlanian guard who had spoken to them, "will be answered, if at all, by Lanis, himself."

"Doctor Lanis," hissed Sam Hubert, watching Shahn.

"He seems to be the leader in this area," observed Shahn, coldly. "But where is the main Metamorph center on Earth?"

"This is Main Base," answered the guard.

"Then—Lanis is your false *Khal*—the top Metamorph?"

"He is."

"Did you hear *that?*" said Hubert, tensely. "This is the main center, Shahn. At last—you have led us to it!"

Shahn's brow furrowed in puzzlement.

"How did I do that? And who is *us?*"

"Don't you understand? For a long time I've had you under observation, hoping you would make them show their hand—even before you called on Dalaney that night in the Hollywoodland Hills. And by *us*—I mean the United States Airforce, chum."

"Hey," exclaimed Wade. "Uncle Sam couldn't know where we are now—or *could* he?"

"You bet your sweet life he does," enthused Hubert. "Those new ships are well equipped. They can trace these tunnels from the air. It's all they needed."

"All they needed?" asked the Nrlanian spokesman. "For what?"

"For planting a good-sized hydrogen bomb. Under these conditions, I don't mind being expendable."

"Holy mackerel," ejaculated Wade, proudly.

Lillian's widened eyes sought Sam's. "They wouldn't?" she gasped, experiencing a shock of claustrophobia.

Shahn thought: He's hedging. He said we must play for time. That bomb remark is merely rhetorical.

Sam shrugged, and the guard laughed.

"You may be expendable," said the latter, "but I doubt if your fair cities of Hollywood and greater Los Angeles are. You are now directly beneath the Hollywoodland Hills. Moreover, we are quite aware of those new planes. They can be eliminated any time we choose."

"I'm afraid not," countered Hubert. "We're familiar with your magnetic disruptors and are completely shielded."

The officer was caught off guard by this remark, as were his five companions. They paled, looking from Hubert to Shahn.

Shahn smiled. "Perhaps I am still the only one who can save your skins now," he said to them. "The Earthmen have caught up to you. As your true *Khal,* I can negotiate through this United States agent—if you will turn your allegiance back into the human path. All is not yet lost to our race. You must decide before it is forever too late."

The guards hesitated, but at last their leader composed himself. "You may have shields against the disrupters," he said, "but not against the *real* weapon. I don't suppose you know that your precious General Morrison is dead."

"General Morrison—of the Strategic Air Command? But—I just talked to him tonight," Hubert insisted.

The guard sneered. "You were speaking to a Metamorph. And *he* is in command of those radiation-engined aircraft, so you see your plans have reversed upon you. You have spared us the necessity of using spacecraft—as the terrestrial craft, are actually in our service, providing us with what in your own tactical jargon is known as an air umbrella against real interference."

"But hey!   Those   pilots   wouldn't   obey   any Metamumpus—or whatever you call it," complained Wade.

"They would obey General Morrison," returned the guard, "and to all appearances he *is* General Morrison. So you see, there is really no defense, Shahn—it is futile—and you, too, must learn to serve the new order."

Lillian burst into tears and threw herself into Shahn's arms. "Shahn...Shahn," she cried out. "Is there no hope left in this world for us? There *has* to be, Shahn. Tell me there is—because the next world is lost forever!"

Shahn held her close, as he flared at the guards. Wade's mouth dropped open in amazement as he observed Lillian. At first, hurt jealousy clouded his eyes. Then his big mouth tightened in resignation.

"Aw, for crying out loud," he blurted out. "I give up. What's next?"

Sam Hubert stared at Shahn in silent deliberation. His thoughts were deep, sharp and inexpressible, for reasons, which he could share with no one at the moment...

CHAPTER NINE
Indoctrination

THE GROUP of captives arrived now at a T-shaped junction of passageways, and here was another disc-gate, before which stood a single Nrlanian in ordinary Terrestrial clothing. His eyes were only on Shahn, and as the latter approached he nodded with a mixed expression of cynicism and feigned deference.

"Welcome, Shahn," he said quietly. "I am instructed to show you something before you see Lanis." The man turned to the guards and said, in Nrlanian, "Take the prisoners to First Stage."

"Wait," demanded Shahn, sharply. "We will not be separated."

The other smiled, with a slight shrug. "We have no need here for melodramatics—no dictatorship. You will find our ways and our purposes quite reasonable. Your friends may accompany you to see what you have to see—but it is a personal thing. If you are willing to be emotionally disrobed, as it were, in public—it is up to you. But I have attempted to spare you that."

Lillian's fear-darkened eyes sought Shahn's, her hand slipping into his, pleadingly. "I'll be with you, Shahn," she murmured.

Wade could only stand there dumbfoundedly watching the two. But Sam Hubert was not to be excluded.

"I'm with you, Shahn," he said. "Let's face it together, whatever it is."

The Nrlanian agent waved his hands in a sign of resignation. He pressed a wall stud, and the disc-gate slid silently into a niche, revealing a seemingly endless passageway.

"Bring them all," he ordered, to the guards. Without further conversation, he led the way.

They had not walked far before he stopped before a small door in the wall of the corridor. He paused, his hand half raised before a small lighted square panel.

"Prepare yourself for a shock," he said, almost coldly. He passed his hand before the lighted square, and the door shot downward into the floor. He pointed inside a dimly lighted chamber, inviting them to enter.

"Watch for a trap," whispered Hubert, placing a restraining hand on Shahn's arm.

The Nrlanian agent smiled faintly.

"Very illogical," he corrected. "If any traps were reserved for you—you might well call your capture, in itself, a trap. You are in our hands. Why elaborate upon an established condition? But—if you insist—" He stepped into the room first.

Shahn, Lillian, Hubert and Wade Kennedy followed, the guards entering behind them.

There was a screen of greenish light. Beyond it, sitting on a crude stone bench before a stone table, was a man—a tall, broad-shouldered man with deep-set gray eyes. On his broad brow was the twin scar symbol of the *Khals.*

"*Vrulnus.*" cried Shahn hoarsely. "Vrulnus!" He rushed forward.

"Stop," cried the Nrlanian agent, stepping in front of him with mercurial swiftness. "The screen will kill you."

Sam Hubert's strong hand was on Shahn's trembling shoulder, steadying him, holding him back.

"Vrulnus," Shahn cried out again. "Beloved *Khal*—I *knew* you lived. I have found you at last. Thanks to Eternity—thanks to Ao—now all things are possible."

Lillian looked wonderingly from Shahn's greenish, sweat-glistening face to the face of the great *Khal* of whom she had heard so much. As Vrulnus lifted up his head to look at them, she saw that his eyes were dull and listless. There was that in his tired face which caused her heart to sink within her.

"Vrulnus. Can't you hear me?" pleaded Shahn. "This is Shahn—your devoted disciple of Nrlan."

Slowly, Vrulnus spoke, in the hollow tones of a hopeless man. "Well do I hear you, Shahn. And I see you there, standing straight and proud as the *Khal* I might have made you. You have found me at last, after the endless years and the terrible journey, and the waiting—the hoping and striving. But this is not victory, Shahn—" Vrulnus' great frame trembled. His gray eyes misted over. "Not victory, Shahn. The olden dream is lost forever. We must do *their* bidding."

Shahn straightened, his eyes blazing a full measure of rage and hate. "What have they done to you?" he cried out. "The dream you taught me, Vrulnus—the secret dream of the race. It is not done—because *I* am here beside you. And we shall *not* do their bidding."

Suddenly, the Nrlanian agent signaled to the guards. "That is all," he said. "We shall leave."

Before the Terrestrials present were aware of Shahn's desperate movement, three of the guards lay senseless on the floor. In the next instant, Shahn was standing there with a sonic heater in each hand, burning the other three guards into ashes.

Lillian lunged toward Wade, groaning in horror, but Wade could only stand there with Hubert, his brows raised in petrified incomprehension. There was a suffocating stench of burned cloth and flesh in the room.

Shahn whirled, his teeth flashing, the heaters aimed at the Nrlanian agent. "Release that screen," he demanded.

"You are overlooking one grave contingency," replied the latter, calmly. As he spoke, he faded from view and a darkening mist gathered in the room.

"A Metamorph," cried Sam Hubert. In the deepening darkness, he bent over, as though trying to find something in his clothing. Then he fell to the floor, as did Lillian and Wade.

Cold vertigo seized Shahn, and he saw nothing momentarily but the bright red glow of the wall where his heavy heaters expended terrible forces. Then he, too, succumbed to an insupportable weight that crushed his mind downward into darkness…

* * *

STAGE ONE was indoctrination. The Communists would have been proud of it, as Wade Kennedy expressed it. All was kindness, cooperation, and "brotherly love." Its outstanding feature was that its activities were devoted principally to the indoctrination of Terrestrials who had been captured on one pretext or another from all walks of life. In fact, many of them were kidnapped public officials whose places in the outer world had been taken over by Metamorphs.

Just why Shahn was subjected to Stage One processing was not quite clear, but Lillian was glad of it because it kept him at her side. Sullen, brooding deeply over his experience with Vrulnus, contemptuous of his captors—he was dangerous, yet he was permitted to attend one of the "meetings" in the Stage One assembly chamber.

The man who addressed them was a city councilman from Chicago. He was big, square-shouldered, beefy, fattened by both propaganda and the fruits thereof.

"He'd be complete," grumbled Wade to Lillian, "if he had boots and a star and crescent."

"Shut up," protested an already indoctrinated listener in a seal behind him. The latter was a square-faced, blunt-fisted truck-driver from San Pedro.

Wade grinned at him. "I been pushed around by these Narlayneeans, buddy, but you're different." His grin faded abruptly. "You keep your yap shut or I'll laminate it."

The man scowled back, but he subsided for a moment. A few other roughs in the same row put their heads together with the truck-driver, nodding darkly toward Wade. Sam Hubert caught Lillian's eye and winked at her. She hung her head, too disorientated and distraught to be mortified. Shahn stared calculatingly at the Terrestrial speaker on the stage.

"Before we advance to Stage Two," announced the latter pontifically, "which is programming our organized activities in the outer world—I'll bring some of the newcomers up to date. Incidentally"— He looked disdainfully at Shahn. "We have an extremely important personage with us tonight, I am not permitted to divulge his identity at present, but I assure you"—sarcastically—"we should be honored and impressed."

Heads turned, faces gawked. Shahn kept his eyes steadfastly on the speaker, stern and expressionless, which only served to emphasize his kingly bearing.

"Now, to summarize," the councilman continued, briskly. "The position of Earthmen with relation to the Nrlanian invasion is quite simply and logically stated. Number one: There is nothing that can be done about the Metamorphs and the mutation. That is a point I'll explain and prove, but it is a premise you will have to accept for the moment. Number two: Only Nrlanians are involved. The Metamorphs demand nothing but our cooperation—whereas they could wipe us off the face of the Earth if they chose to do so. Number three: The single objective of the Metamorphs is to find the hidden Nrlanians—everywhere—round them up, and organize them for the mutation they must go through eventually, anyway, because they're built that way. In this task, they are enlisting the aid of Earthmen. Number four: In exchange for our cooperation they will gradually place collaborators in advantageous positions of power and influence—"

"You lie!"

All eyes turned to see Shahn rise slowly to his feet with clenched fists, his nostrils distended in rage.

"You're a pusillanimous, ignorant, fattened, expendable tool of master minds," he shouted through his teeth. "You know nothing about it. Look ahead, Earthman. Look ahead at the time when you will have aided the Metamorphs in fully achieving their purpose. Given perfect conditions, they will multiply through accelerated mutation and they will be *hungry*—millions of them!" He turned swiftly, glaring at the assembly. "Do you know what constitutes *food* for the Metamorphs—? For your so benevolent masters?"

He stopped, looking about him dumbfoundedly. Everyone, including Lillian, Wade, and Sam Hubert, was holding his head as though in pain. When he stopped, however, the source of their pain abated.

"Mister Meade," said the speaker, quietly.

Shahn turned and glared at him.

"Just as there are sounds, which are audible to your ears alone, so there are sounds in the lower audibility range of Terrestrials that you do not register. This particular combination of discords is very painful to Earthly ears. Unfortunately, your voice was drowned out, as you are not permitted to speak here. Your time will come—so please bear with us, hmm?"

Shahn said nothing more, considering the man on the stage unworthy of his further attention. He sat down, resolved to wait his turn.

"Why, the dirty sonofa—" Wade started to say.

"Shut up!!!" came a chorus from the rear.

Wade turned to face five rough-looking characters instead of one. He smiled, fascinated. Almost with a childish expression of curiosity, he reached out and tweaked the San Pedro man's nose with artistic and studied deliberation.

"Wade," Lillian hissed at him.

Two men instantly grabbed Wade and the largest one of the five rose to strike him. Wade let out a war whoop and leapt into the row behind him. He flattened two of his tormentors with as many blows. More joined in, but then Sam Hubert went into battle.

When the Nrlanian guards, dull-witted *drals,* came running into the assembly chamber, Shahn rose up in hungering wrath. Bedlam ensued, until suddenly a siren sounded and a blinding light flashed intermittently from the stage.

Wade, Sam and Shahn paused over prostrate foes to observe the presence of three blue-uniformed true Nrlanian guardsmen there, one of whom was an officer. The latter held in his hand a Nrlanian torch beam, which he snapped off when he had gained everyone's attention. On either side of him, his companions held sonic heaters aimed at the assembly.

"Order," shouted the officer, scowling. "Or be burned down at once—do you hear?"

Shahn stepped forward unhesitatingly and came to a stop below the stage, facing them. "This farce has gone far enough," he snapped at them, imperiously. "You know who I am. Take me to Lanis at once!"

The officer sneered down at him. "Yes, I know who you are. Great Lanis, *Khal* of the Metamorphs, has been busy elsewhere. He will see you now."

"Wait a minute," said Hubert, coming up behind Shahn. "Believe me, Shahn, it is vital that I go with you. Bargain for it."

"Don't leave me here, Shahn," pleaded Lillian, running to his side and clinging to his arm.

"How about me?" grinned Wade, striding up, sporting a proud shiner and a missing tooth.

Shahn looked at his three companions gravely, then up at the officers. "They will accompany me," he said.

"I don't think—" the officer began.

"Correct," snapped Shahn. "You *don't* think. You obey. You all want something, which even the Metamorphs seek in me—the *sarniall*. Well, do as I say or take my corpse. I am done. Now lead the way…"

The dumbfounded survivors of the brawl on the assembly hall stared from Shahn to the officer, including the rather pasty-hued councilman from Chicago. The Nrlanian tensed, pressed his lips together, then turned abruptly.

"Follow me," he said.

The guards with the heaters stepped aside, their weapons trained on Shahn.

"Come on," said Shahn, and his companions fell in wordlessly behind him.

WHILE en route to their new destination, Sam Hubert caught Wade's private ear for a word of advice.

"Wade, you're a war veteran. You've seen combat, haven't you?"

"Yeah. So?"

"In a defended position, why is it the small arms and light artillery are usually fired first?"

"That's easy. The big guns hold fire until they're needed, so's to conceal their positions."

"Exactly. In a way, you're a big gun, defense-wise. Did you notice in that fight back there that quite a few were on *our* side?"

"I didn't have time. Were there some?"

"Yes. This thing can be split wide open—perhaps not soon, but eventually."

"No kidding. So I'm a big gun, am I?"

"Consider it that way. Hold your fire until the right time, lest you attract the heaviest fire of the enemy prematurely. Don't be conspicuous. Hold your tongue and your temper—but keep your eyes and ears open."

Wade scratched his head. "By that token, you must be atomic ordnance. Boy! Did *you* lay those guys out fast. Say, what about that H-bomb business? Do you think—"

"We're not out of *that* danger yet." Sam clapped him on the shoulder. "Quiet, friend. Here we are."

They were admitted into a dimly illuminated room, which was richly appointed, with deep carpeting and upholstered furniture. Save for the total absence of books, it might have been a private study in a wealthy home. There was a wide-top mahogany desk and a tall-backed leather swivel chair—empty.

"I don't like this room," whispered Lillian.

"That's understandable," returned Hubert. "We are in the presence of another Metamorph—perhaps Lanis." Shahn looked at him sharply. "How do you know that?"

Hubert shrugged. "I've seen this kind of dimness in a room before. So have you."

In that moment, the lamps in the room brightened, and simultaneously the tenuous darkness condensed in the direction of the swivel chair. Lillian gripped both Shahn and Wade, trying not to cry out, as the three dimensional, faceless shadow of a man materialized behind the desk. Then she did cry out as the shadow became that same little cherubic-faced man with the twinkling blue eyes and the goatee whom she had seen capture Shahn at the hospital.

"Doctor Lanis," she exclaimed, horrified.

Lanis waved his hands in a most cheerful and disarming manner. "I did that deliberately," he said, "to prove a point. The point is—there is no camouflage here. We will face only the truth. I am a Metamorph. As such, my objectives are clearly defined—my terms with regard to yourselves are simple and just. You are here to learn what they are."

"I know what they are," said Shahn, coldly. "You want the *sarniall*—and the lives of my friends here is the price you offer."

"Correct in the first part—wrong as to the latter," replied Lanis.

"But—if the Metamorphs want the *sarniall*," put in Lillian, "why don't they get it from Vrulnus, who was its original inventor?"

"A point I was going to make, myself," added Hubert.

"We tried," said Lanis, expressionlessly. "But our only persuasion, in this case, was mental and physical torture. He broke, mentally. He seems incapable of building the *sarniall* now."

Shahn's face hardened under the strain of controlling his emotions. "Leave Vrulnus alone," he said. "I can buy *his* freedom, you may have the *sarniall* and myself, as well."

Wade frowned at Shahn. "Hey! You mean you'd play ball with these Metamuppuses?"

"Silence," commanded, Lanis. "Shahn, I will get to the point. There is no need to threaten you or your companions with death, as the alternative. Capable people are always worth more alive than dead—to any cause. But here is my proposition. I want the *sarniall*. Build it, and your reward shall be precisely this: Vrulnus and yourself free—but exiled from Earth. We'll give you a star ship and the time necessary to locate a desirable objective in some other solar system."

Lillian, who still held on to Shahn's arm, felt him tense.

"And the alternative?" he asked.

Lanis shrugged. "We shall perform further experiments upon Vrulnus. He may be able to work under hypnosis. If our method fails, he may become a raving lunatic."

Shahn looked at his companions. "A dilemma fiendish enough to become classical," he commented, gravely, his eyes mostly on Lillian. "My prime objective has been to find Vrulnus, and now to rescue him. Yet, the price for this is to make the Metamorphs invulnerable. This is equivalent to offering them Earth on a platter—in exchange for Vrulnus."

"That is about the size of it," put in Sam Hubert. "What do you choose, Shahn?"

His eyes were still on Lillian when he answered. "I choose—Vrulnus."

Lanis smiled. Hubert remained expressionless, watching the Metamorph. Lillian's eyes never left Shahn's, but she cried silently, looking at him.

"Well," said Wade, abruptly, *"that* separates the men from the boys. You're a traitor to Earth, Shahn. They can do with me what they want, but you can count me on the other side—*my* side. I hate your guts."

Sam Hubert cleared his throat. "Lanis," he said, "I am a physicist. Since Shahn's decision in this matter seems irrevocable, the damage is already done. Therefore, I'd like to earn the right to become an exile on that star ship. I am volunteering to be Shahn's assistant. After all, I'm familiar with sources of special materials, scientific equipment, and the like…"

"Quisling," cried Lillian, as she slapped Sam Hubert's face.

"Lil," said Wade, putting his arm around her. "To each his own, baby. Don't waste your strength."

Lillian broke into uncontrollable sobbing. "You don't understand, Wade. You don't…understand…"

He had to hold her in his arms to keep her from falling to the floor. As Shahn stood there looking at Sam Hubert and at Lanis, his face was a colorless mask of death…

Hubert walked over and put his hand on Shahn's shoulder, facing Lillian. "Lillian," he said, quietly, "I'm afraid it is *you* who do not understand."

She looked up at him, startled, resentful, through streaming tears. Shahn watched Hubert warily.

"I would ask you," said the latter, carefully, "to examine the meaning of courage—which is to hold on, and to strive, beyond the boundaries of hope." He glared at her meaningfully. "I believe you have that courage."

When Shahn looked again at Lillian, their eyes met—and held.

Wade wrinkled his brow in puzzlement and muttered, "Huh?"

CHAPTER TEN
Rospor

SHAHN wiped sweat off his emaciated brow. He looked across the lab assembly bench at Sam Hubert.

"Just who the hell *are* you?" he demanded.

Hubert switched off an oscilloscope and disconnected it from the nearly completed *sarniall*. He raised his brows in mild surprise.

"What brought all that on?" he asked.

"You know who I am. Of course, we haven't had the leisure to go into all of my past—but I was a nuclear physicist before I—ah—became vitally interested in flying saucers."

The long weeks of pressure and worry about Lillian had drained Shahn visibly. The girl and Wade had been sent back to Stage One, and he and Hubert had been isolated in the laboratory area.

"I'm not insensitive or stupid," retorted Shahn, glaring at him. "You have a hidden motive in helping me with the *sarniall*. You're an abnormally brilliant scientist, and you're too clever to wear real motives on your sleeve. The connection with the U. S. Airforce Intelligence is a cover-up."

Hubert took a big breath. He gave Shahn a warning frown, reminding him of a previous agreement they had made to avoid vital topics. The lab, he was sure, must be "bugged."

"All right," he lied, cheerfully. "I'll come clean with you, Shahn. I've been trying to get hold of a flying saucer. Sound silly?"

Shahn studied him a moment, not knowing just how far he was carrying the camouflage for the possible delusion of monitors—or of himself.

"Perhaps not," he shrugged. "It would mean a lot to terrestrial science."

"But I want it for myself. This world needs new horizons. I want to visit Earth's neighboring planets."

"I see. And as a substitute for your personal objective, you seek to become an exile with Vrulnus and myself—but we are not interested in your neighboring planets, Mars is dying of old age. Venus is a steaming, smouldering infant. The rest are dead or unborn."

"All the better, then, that I should visit the stars with you."

Shahn frowned a warning at Hubert. "And never see Earth again?"

Hubert galled about the lab surreptitiously. "Don't you intend to return again—for vengeance?"

Accident or deliberate plant? Shahn wondered at his strange companion. Quite loudly and clearly, he replied, "That would be futile. Soon the Metamorphs will have established themselves as the dominant mutation here. In a way, it isn't their fault. It is the same process of Nature which placed *homo sapiens* here as the dominant mutation over the apes. This is only one small planet lost in Infinity. Vrulnus and I can find another home."

"It would be worth the rest of my life to help you find it, Shahn."

Shahn returned to his work. "Then we'll have to earn that trip and finish the weapon. The sooner the better. There's no use fighting against the local situation here on Earth. I am done with it."

Both men fell to work in silence, realizing that they had not answered a single question in their minds with respect to each other. It had all been for the benefit of their captors, should they be eavesdropping. The principal question in Hubert's mind was: He's bringing this weapon rapidly to completion.

What are his plans when he actually finishes it? Does he really intend giving it to the enemy?

Shahn wondered much about Hubert, but in his own mind there was no major question—only an unfamiliar prayer to unknown Ao: That Lillian was safe, and that the Metamorphs would refrain from tampering further with the fabulous mind of Vrulnus. There were certain priceless secrets still extant in that noble cranium—without which his own dream of life and hope was dead.

Both he and Sam Hubert shared one conviction in common. At the moment the *sarniall* was ready, the enemy would be there to receive it. If any counteraction was planned, it would have to occur at that precise moment.

STAGE TWO indoctrinates were allowed to use the visiscopes. Wade and Lillian had already looked upon Hollywood in the screens. They could not help but wonder at the blindness of the outer world, which blandly carried on its complex, materialistic existence oblivious to the doom that was being prepared for it.

But one night they discovered a startling change in the outer world. They were with a small group, unaccompanied by their tutors, for whom they had been instructed to wait. To kill time, Wade turned on the scope, and the huge screen on the wall came to life.

"Hey," he exclaimed. "Looks like an air raid."

Lillian looked up listlessly to see searchlights combing the skies of Hollywood and Los Angeles.

"If it's an air raid," commented a weather-wizened rancher from Ventura, "what good are searchlights? Even radar would be short notice these days."

"Can't be advertising," said another. "Not like that—all over town."

Wade flipped on the sound system at low volume, and at once they heard the mournful wail of sirens. Everybody looked at each other significantly.

"It *must* be an emergency of some kind," said Lillian, finally. "Can you magnify the screen, Wade?"

Wade spun a dial, and Vine Street leapt at them in full detail. They observed the intersection of Sunset and Vine. The streets were overcrowded with traffic, but it was a kind of traffic they had not witnessed before—not, at least, at Sunset and Vine.

Buses, trucks, autos, motorcycles—even bicycles towing makeshift trailers—moved slowly between military trucks, weapons carriers and jeeps. Every vehicle available moved toward the Hollywood Freeway, filled to maximum capacity, with men, women, children, and personal belongings. Still more people fought to find room in the public vehicles, pulling out bundles and articles of furniture to get in. The sidewalks were littered with cast-off items, and the yelling masses clambered over them heedlessly, watching for their chance to get transportation on the outbound freeway, toward Pomona, Santa Ana, Pasadena, El Monte—anywhere, just so it was out of Hollywood.

Wade whistled. "They aren't just practicing," he said. "That's wholesale evacuation if I ever saw it."

Lillian clutched at his arm. "But why, Wade? Why?"

He shrugged. "You heard what Sam Hubert said about an H-bomb. Maybe the big brass is afraid it might happen."

"We gotta get outta here," wailed an aging blonde woman who might have been a B-girl in her time. "It ain't safe!"

While a general tumult arose and people began to plead with the *dral* guards to let them go, Wade stared thoughtfully at the scene on the screen.

"It might not be so safe here, at that," he muttered. "The objective wouldn't be the city—it would be the Metamumps—their buried crystals or whatever you call them."

Lillian watched Wade's face, fascinated by a mounting fear. "Chrysalides," she corrected. "That's exactly it, Wade. And who could know this is their Main Base but Sam Hubert? Wade—somehow, Sam Hubert is directing an attack on this place."

"What are you talking about? How could he?"

"I don't know—but he is."

"Uh, oh. Instincts again. They never fail…"

"Then *believe* me, Wade. We've got to find him."

"What for? I think it's a good idea to blast this creep joint off the map."

"But Shahn. We must warn him."

"That no good, chicken—"

"Wade, please. You don't know—it means *more* than life to *me.*"

Wade's temper burst its bonds. "You're nuts," he fumed. "For once you're gonna do it my way. We're busting out." He turned to a half dozen men who had been watching the screen, and to others who were arguing with the guards. "Hey! You want out—follow me!" He pulled Lillian with him, and the men followed. Briefly, he let go of her, as he threw himself on the men surrounding the guards, pushing them on top of the *drals.* "Smother those guys," he yelled. "Get their guns!"

The six men with him dog-piled the mass of humanity pressing upon the *drals,* and the latter were incapacitated by the sheer weight of numbers.

Wade piled in over their shoulders and came up with a sonic heater. He waved it over his head and grabbed Lillian again. "Come on," he yelled. "Don't stop for anything! Just keep going!"

THE FINAL assembly of the *sarniall* had been arranged for a very special audience in the Main Base conference chamber. The *sarniall,* devoid of its final activating circuit assembly, lay on a table before three tiers of seats. On these latter sat a group of men who might have just walked out of the New York Stock Exchange—distinguished looking citizens all. Yet they were leading Metamorphs.

Their leader, Lanis, sat on a raised dais before a broad desk, but not in human form. He was a dense, faceless man-shadow.

At the assembly table stood Shahn and Hubert. Beside the *sarniall* were several small parts awaiting assembly. At a sign from dark Lanis, a guard handed Shahn a Nrlanian welder, powered by the same "infra-battery," which Shahn had sold to the Jonathan Corporation.

"Begin the final assembly," ordered Lanis, in hollow, sepulchral tones. "But remember this—one false move, and you, alone, Shahn, know how you will die."

Boldly, Hubert asked aloud, almost ingenuously, "How will we die, Shahn?"

Shahn was already at work. "As food," he said, just as boldly. "This is a room full of Metamorphs."

"You mean—" Sam looked up at the assemblage of distinguished-looking gentlemen. "Our flesh?"

"No."

"Then *what?*"

"Have you ever heard of the *elan vital?*"

"Silence," commanded Lanis.

In that moment, however, five Nrlanian guards pushed into the chamber led by a Metamorph shadow. With them were two struggling prisoners.

Shahn looked up, tensing. "Lillian. Wade."

"Seize Shahn and his terrestrial accomplice," cried the newly arrived Metamorph. "This is an emergency."

Lanis' shadow rose up in macabre silence and stood there as guards pulled Shahn and Hubert away from the table.

"Explain yourself, Ralnor," said Lanis, evenly.

"The outside is being evacuated. A hydrogen bomb attack is feared. These two—" He indicated Lillian and Wade. "Have knowledge of it, which involves this Earthman, Hubert. They are also guilty of inciting a riot and inadvertently broke into the *crypt.*"

Wade, ragged and dirty, snarling hate, yelled at Hubert. "It's their tomb. All their crystals are in there—" A guard struck him and he staggered.

Lillian, equally disheveled but somehow wildly determined to resist, now that she saw Shahn, cried out, "And there's a giant star ship!"

Shahn waited no longer. He broke free, leapt to the table and slapped the small welded circuit assembly into the *sarniall.* A heat ray crackled, but Lanis shouted, "No!" In the instant that the sonic heater clicked off, Lanis assumed human form—but not the form of the cherubic faced little man.

Towering before them was Vrulnus, himself.

"Shahn," he said, smiling sardonically into the teeth of the *sarniall,* "would you destroy your *Khal?*"

"You—" cried Shahn, incredulously. "A Metamorph!"

"The same as the one you talked to so touchingly in his prison cell. What of our dream of life now, Shahn?"

Lillian held her temples, trying not to break. Her widened eyes could not leave that noble face that deceived the mind and the senses.

"It was a trick," snarled Shahn. "You are not Vrulnus—never were."

"Then perhaps *this* you will believe," said the image of Vrulnus. *"This* I really was when you knew me last."

When the shape of Vrulnus changed to that of a tall, thin man, Shahn could only remember the other's murderous laughter on another world centuries before, when Sralna had died in the grip of a Metamorph.

"Rospor!" he shouted, forgetting the *sarniall* entirely. With a choking cry of murderous rage, he sprang for the dais…

CHAPTER ELEVEN
Death Stand

SHAHN landed in the spot, which had been occupied by Rospor, but it was empty. The entire assemblage of distinguished looking gentlemen had dissolved into swirling shadows that now converged upon him with a cold cloying touch of death beyond death—and Shahn, paralyzed, began to lose the color of life.

"Shahn!" screamed Lillian. She broke loose from the guards and ran to him, clinging to him in spite of the indescribable horror of the death that embraced them both.

Wade Kennedy struggled mightily in the grip of the five guards, shouting hoarsely. "Lillian! For the love of God—no!"

"Away," shouted Sam Hubert, suddenly picking up the *sarniall* and running to the dais. He activated it, taking care to aim its dark forces above the slumping bodies of Shahn and Lillian.

Instantly, most of the chilling death shadows swirled away from the deadly area, yet one great shadow held stubbornly to the bodies of its two victims. Sam Hubert stepped deliberately within the influence of the Metamorph, the while he reached for his artificial leg. With his bare hand, he tore apart his trouser leg, and there was revealed a glistening instrument of steel, wire and glowing tubes. Surprised and suddenly wary of its life, the single remaining Metamorph dissolved into nothingness. Before the Nrlanian guards could bring their heaters to bear on Hubert, the entire dais was surrounded by a pale blue shield of energy.

At his feet, Shahn and Lillian revived slowly, looking about them, mystified, at the dome of energy, which protected them. Shahn struggled weakly to his feet, pulling Lillian up with him. His eyes went for Hubert, alone, as the latter, grimy, holding the *sarniall* in his hands, impeded the deeper shadows of the council chamber.

"Who are you?" asked Shahn.

"Guards," shouted Hubert in a new, deep tone of authority. "You have witnessed the power of your *Khal.*" Wherewith, he tore from his forehead a strip of false flesh, and there gleamed forth the twin white scars of Vrulnus, *Khal* of Nrlan.

"*Vrulnus,*" cried Shahn. "Vrulnus—at last!"

Lillian stared, dry-eyed, then buried her head in Shahn's willing arms. Relief came in a tidal wave as devastating as all the fears and torments which had preceded it.

The true Nrlanian guards in the room lowered their weapons and, instinctively, they kneeled down.

"Vrulnus," exclaimed their commanding officer. "Forgive us. We thought you were dead. Without you, great *Khal,* there was no hope…"

"But—Vrulnus," protested Shahn, overcome by the confusion of his mixed emotions. "You hid your identity from *me.* Why?"

"There is no time, Shahn. That bomb threat is real. Come on. Stay within my shield."

As he moved, the shield moved with him, generated by the marvelous instrument in his artificial limb. "Guards," he ordered, "you will recruit your forces—scatter among the peoples of the Earth—and resist the work of the Metamorphs until I return."

"But where will you go, *Khal?*" asked the leading officer.

"That is my secret. I have but waited to find my own ship, which Rospor stole from me on Nrlan. It is in the *crypt.* Thanks to you, Wade Kennedy, my time for action did not come too late."

"Well—whatever the hell's going on count me in," said Wade.

Abruptly, the energy shield dropped. Vrulnus stepped to Wade's side, and the shield reappeared.

"Stay inside this," said Vrulnus, "in case *they* return."

"You mean the Metamumps can't get through this?"

"They cannot. Now tell me—where is the crypt of the chrysalides and my ship?"

WITH the advent of the genuine Vrulnus, the aspect of the world seemed to change. Shahn walked proud and straight behind him, and his grip on Lillian's hand was firm and confident. Wade Kennedy, leading the way with the Nrlanian guards, called cheerfully to every fugitive Terrestrial who chanced to run into their path.

"Join the parade. The war's over. Come on!"

Other Nrlanians who would have opposed them quickly recognized their undisputed leader and turned their allegiance to him. Sporadic attacks on the part of the Metamorph conditioned drals were met with a withering fire on the part of the loyalist forces that were swiftly gathering. By the time they neared the crypt, their party numbered nearly a hundred of mixed Terrestrials and Nrlanians.

"Are we getting out of here?" some of them asked.

"What about the H-bomb?"

"Who's this big guy with the 'space gun' in his hands?"

"I don't get it, but if this gets us out, count me in!"

"Where are the Metamorphs all this time?"

Wade turned and shouted to all Terrestrials present. "You jokers take it easy. Follow the leader close now—this ain't no picnic yet. The Metamumps have gone back into their shells—in this tomb ahead."

Some who could not dominate their fear of the Metamorphs dropped out of the group at this point. The rest quieted down, watching Vrulnus in wondering fear and hope.

"I'm sorry about your leg," Shahn said to the *Khal.* "How did it happen?"

Vrulnus gripped the *sarniall* tightly, looking ahead. "It was no accident," he answered. "It was high-priced surgery."

Shahn looked abruptly at Lillian, then back at Vrulnus, incredulous. "You mean—you—"

Vrulnus cut him off with a piercing surveillance. "How *else* was I to smuggle my weapon into the enemy's midst?"

Words deserted Shahn. He could not have done justice to his admiration for his leader's iron courage and will. He and Lillian followed the great *Khal* in silent awe and enraptured deference.

Shahn had a thousand questions on his lips, but just now there loomed before them a lightless tunnel mouth in the depths of the Metamorph lair. A disc-gate at the entrance had been melted apart by sonic heaters.

"It lights up—kinda," said Wade, "after you get into it. Then there's a giant cave—" He gulped once, looking at Vrulnus. "And that's the place."

"The crypt of the chrysalides," muttered someone fearfully.

"The Metamorphs waiting in their graves…"

"Their backs against the wall."

"They'll fight, won't they?"

"Hey, I'm getting out of here!"

Vrulnus turned slowly to face them all. His gray eyes seemed to search each sub-cellar of their minds. "You are all indispensable," he said. "You of Nrlan are experienced. You know the strength of the Metamorph and you have seen my strength. You are now my own chosen deputies on Earth. You will establish secret connections with the rest of our kind and form cells of resistance until I return.

"You Terrestrials are also experienced. You know now what danger threatens you. You will form an alliance with my people to fight your common foe. Your fight will be a delaying action until I return prepared for the final battle. But just now—at least these shall be destroyed." He nodded his head toward the tunnel.

Without further speech, he turned and entered the forbidding shadows. Slowly, the others followed, while Shahn, Lillian and Wade remained close beside the great man, remembering his protective energy shield.

"You can't kill a Metamorph," somebody complained.

"This guy can. That gun—it destroys their projections, anyway," said another.

"But not their shells. Nothing can destroy a chrysalide."

"Not even an H-bomb?"

"Hey! How about that?"

Once more, the deep voice of Vrulnus was heard in the dimness of the tunnel. "I am controlling that," he answered. "But we must hurry."

"Hurry? To what? There's no exit down here."

"There must be. My ship is here."

"Good. Then why hurry, if you're running the whole show?"

"Don't forget—there are other Metamorph bases—and other Nrlanian Ships. My pilots cannot shield us indefinitely from outside attack."

Shahn could not suppress his curiosity. *"Your* pilots? But I thought—General Morrison—"

"I have used my years well on Earth, Shahn, preparing for this moment. Those Airforce pilots are Nrlanians—my own men. The moment I was told Morrison had been replaced by a Metamorph, I took direct command."

Shahn thought: *How?*

And Vrulnus' own powerful thought returned: *Have you forgotten, Shahn?*

"Telepathy," he blurted out.

The conversation was getting beyond the comprehension of the multitude that followed. A child-like, trustful silence on their part ensued, except for one insuppressible reaction.

"I think, I'm gonna flip…"

In the darkness, Wade's gravel-toned voice was readily recognized by Shahn and Lillian. They caught themselves smiling incongruously in the sub-cellars of hell.

Abruptly, the dimly illuminated crypt opened before them…

THE giant cave arched above their heads into impenetrable shadows. Its floor fell away into a broad basin some fifty feet below them. Dimly seen in the distance was the shadowy hull of a giant star ship.

But in between them and their goal, on the floor of the cave, lay fully thirty black, gleaming chrysalides, swollen, petrified caricatures of the human form. Lillian gasped, eyes wide in fascinated horror, biting her knuckles in an effort to stifle a scream.

"God preserve us," someone whispered.

"The living shells of the Metamorphs," said Vrulnus. "Inside—their negative duality, which they can project. Was there ever such a curse in the universe?"

"Kill them," shrieked a woman behind him, in instinctive revulsion. *"Kill them!"*

"Stand back," cried Shahn. "They're coming out!"

He felt Lillian's nails dig involuntarily into his flesh as she saw what he was witnessing. Swirling shadows, like mists of night, rose up from the motionless chrysalides. They seemed to dance in a slow rhythm, like nameless monsters out of the unvisited pits of delirium. As the rhythm increased, the shadows deepened and coalesced into a menacing black cloud. The cave began to lose its proportions.

"Hypnosis," warned Vrulnus, speaking to Wade, Lillian and Shahn. "Stand close."

As they did so, he activated the weapon in his artificial limb, and the blue screen of force surrounded them. Immediately, the insidious mental grip was released, and they saw the cave in its normal proportions.

Then Vrulnus raised the sarniall deliberately and fired. Its dark aura of energy penetrated the screen and went swirling out toward the angry cloud of blackness, wreaking havoc.

Suddenly, the Metamorph shadows were gone. In their place, at Vrulnus' feet beyond the screen, was a group of innocent young women, naked, beautiful, some of them held little infants to their breasts. They held out their arms, or their babies, pleading for life.

"Stop," cried a man's voice behind Vrulnus. "Don't kill them."

The rest of the unshielded crowd, fully hypnotized, tried to push forward against the bluish shield of energy, but were repelled. Within the shield, Vrulnus and his companions saw the illusion only if they willed it. But they could also see within each angelic female form the hovering shadow of a Metamorph.

Remorselessly, Vrulnus fired the *sarniall* at them. Illusion dismembered the young women horribly and spilled apparent life's blood onto the ground.

"Kill them," pleaded Lillian. *"Kill* them!"

The mighty weapon in Vrulnus' hands gradually wiped the illusion away and brought death to the last of the Metamorph extensions. There lay before them only the helpless, physical chrysalides, which nothing could destroy short of atomic fire. Lillian shuddered in revulsion when she knew she shared one thing in common with those hell-spawned monstrous crystals—for they, too, in a sense, had lost their souls.

CHAPTER TWELVE
Concept Incredible

SHAHN and Lillian looked out the visiport of the giant star ship, lost in thought. Astern, Earth's blue-green globe diminished almost visibly in diameter.

"There is so much that has gone unanswered," said Lillian, at last. "When will he tell us?"

"Soon," said Shahn. "We may not have seen the last of the enemy ships. He'll not come out of his shell until danger is past."

"Please don't use that word, Shahn."

"Shell? Yes, I'm sorry. It has acquired a repulsive meaning."

"Shahn—that bomb. It was horrible. Did he have to? I mean—Hollywood, the beautiful hills—all that property—"

"He saw to it the populace was warned in time. What's property now, with what still faces terrestrial civilization? Those chrysalides—their Main Base and the ships—they *had* to go, Lillian."

"It's hard to adjust one's perspective to the reality of the situation. I'm glad, though, he rescued all those people and set them down in a safe place. Do you think they will carry out his instructions?"

"I think so. That last episode in the crypt should have convinced them of what they're up against with other Metamorphs still loose in the world and able to increase their number through Nrlanian mutations." After a moment, he added. "At least I know your good pal, Wade Kennedy, will do his part. He'll lead the opposition if anyone will."

Lillian smiled wistfully. "Poor Wade. He was so loyal, so brave—and loveable. I hope I shall live to see him again."

"You may."

"Oh Shahn—will Vrulnus really go back someday to Earth, prepared to rescue it?"

"I'm sure he intends to."

"But how? Where is he going now?"

"I'm not too sure, but—"

"But what? Tell me, Shahn."

He smiled. "Let's wait and see. Incidentally, you're forgetting something important."

"What is that?" She looked at him wonderingly.

"How much we have to be thankful for."

She smiled, drawing close to him. "Have I forgotten that?"

His lips found hers, and sweet oblivion cast its cloak about them—until he felt her tears against his face. He looked at her, frowning, and dark memory of the *sarniall* returned.

"If I could be whole again," she sobbed. "Oh Shahn— Shahn— How can even Vrulnus return the eternal essence to my finite flesh?"

"There is much we have to ask of him," he answered. "It is why he is such a precious man—a single human with the memory of a world's past greatness and the answers to our dream of life all locked up in his heart and mind. For example, you forget that as a Nrlanian I carry also the seed of mutation—"

Realization came slowly, but Lillian's eyes finally widened in horrified comprehension. "You mean—you, too, could become a—"

He nodded darkly. "It was cowardly of me to mention it to you, yet—the thought might have occurred to you when you were alone. I wanted to tell you this, dearest: Vrulnus has intimated that he has an answer to that problem, too. Can you understand why I was willing to barter a world for his salvation?"

* * *

VRULNUS opened the subject, himself, hours later. "We are safe," he told them, as he emerged from the control room. Somehow, a new zest for life and the glow of constructive energy had added youth to his face, almost obliterating the effect of the scars that had disfigured it. In his deep, gray eyes shone a purpose and confidence—a great expectancy of fulfillment—which was contagious. "Sit down. The time has come for explanations."

They sat on hiberbunks while the giant star ship hurtled with undiminished acceleration out of the solar system.

"This is my own ship," he began. "No one but myself knew its secrets. Rospor stole it from me and I have been helpless without it ever since. He, like the rest of you, Shahn, took several centuries to reach Earth, under suspended animation. Yet this was ironical, for had he known its secret he could have covered the same distance in ten years or less."

"But how is that possible?" protested Shahn. "The mass-energy coordinates curve to infinity at the speed of light. Even Terrestrials know that."

Vrulnus waved his hand impatiently. "Never mind that now. It involves a new type of math relative to the acceleration of Inertia—which is a new concept. We'll get to it later. The important things, we have the ship. Your minds, I can see, are filled with questions, which I will answer.

"Before landing on Earth in an ordinary star ship, I knew what to expect, because my ship was a relatively late arrival too, and I had listened to the tapes. I had already prepared my crew to form the nucleus of an underground organization of resistance to the Metamorphs. It was difficult, even then, to foresee the magnitude of our problem. Our people were scattered; fearful, disguised. I began secretly to organize, but then one night I examined an abandoned ship and was surprised by a force of the enemy I never saw."

He pointed again at the scar on his face. "I was incapacitated for years and even suffered from a partial amnesia. I recovered most of my memory, but still could not remember the most important thing of all—which was the nuclearstatic equation for the field converter of the *sarniall*. Without that, I could not build the weapon.

"I needed you, Shahn, but also I needed my ship. I knew that if it still existed Rospor would have it, and I knew Rospor would be connected with the center of Metamorph control. If I were to reveal my true identity prematurely I would meet with opposition before I was prepared for it. When you finally did arrive, I heard of your clever escape from the Metamorph trap at N-1 Base. I trailed you, hoping that you would attract high level Metamorph attention, and I prepared daily to follow you into their trap—which I finally did.

"I, too, needed money for research—hence my pretended 'discovery' of the radiation engine, which the U.S. Airforce now has. With the money, I developed the sub-energy field generator." He slapped his artificial limb. "This was the surprise I held in reserve for the Metamorphs against the time when you should build a *sarniall*. Well—you know the rest of *that*. I left your *sarniall* with our resistance forces on Earth, knowing that they and your good friend, Wade Kennedy, would put it to good use—perhaps find a way of duplicating and mass-producing it. But now we come to the important part of the discussion."

He paused, smiling at both of them.

"It was the Earthman's strange and startling concept of duality, which finally enabled me to solve the mystery of Ao. And therein lies the answer, I hope, to all our problems at the present moment."

Lillian's brows furrowed in puzzlement. "What is Ao?" she asked.

Shahn was too emotionally involved in these revelations for which he had hungered so long. He could not speak. Vrulnus studied his disciple as though preparing himself for a monumental task.

"It is something almost impossible to explain, because the semantics of the subject are so poorly developed in any living language," he said, at length. "But you shall see it."

"What?" exclaimed Shahn. "You mean—"

Vrulnus nodded. "The real reason behind my urgent need for recovering this ship," he said. "We must return to Ao, and quickly, too. We destroyed Nrlan, but not its moons. I have reason to believe that ancient Gral still circles our double sun in some kind of orbit, however eccentric it may be."

Lillian shook her head, confused. "I'm lost," she said. "Utterly lost."

Shahn gripped her hand in his, bidding her be still. "All right. So we return—and to Ao. *Then* what?"

"First—a bit of theory and Nrlanian history," said Vrulnus. "Not all of our ancient history is known to

Nrlanians except to most of us elders of the generation of Gral. We who walked beneath its dark disc pondered long over the mystery of Ao, and our dead great past. Once, the Nrlani were kings of the universe, but then—tragedy fell upon them. Someone discovered the ether and performed an uncontrolled experiment."

He looked at Lillian. "On Earth, your scientists merely postulated the existence of an unknown substance, *ether*, to explain wave phenomena such as light and magnetics. On Nrlan, they actually identified this so-called ether as a finer matter co-existing in an interlocked balance with gross matter. Ever since your famous 'Manhattan Project' in Chicago, during, which your first nuclear reactor was put to the test, your nuclear physicists have been vaguely aware of what I am driving at, but they have not yet developed the techniques for measuring this sub-matter effectively."

He took a big breath, then said, "It is the substance of which the soul is composed."

Lillian looked at Shahn, remembering the episode in the Church. He had said that if he had a soul he would photograph it. Now she knew what he meant.

"Then—actually what you are saying is that the soul is a *physical* reality?" she queried. She also remembered Shahn's mysterious contention that there was nothing supernatural.

Vrulnus smiled faintly. "Among all races of men and in all times," he replied, "Man, in general, has been possessed of a miraculous inner eye—a Third Eye, so to speak—which has at least perceived the shape of truth when the mere electro-chemical orientation of conscious thought to environment remained inadequate to the task. The result of this inner sight has usually been manifested in the form of a religion, which is an organized social effort to interpret the unknown. I would not offend your faith, Lillian; and on the contrary I can support it. You see, almost all religions had one truth in common—the awareness of co-existence between a gross matter and a finer matter, which phenomenon you refer to as duality.

"To answer your question, then. Has the soul a physical reality? In Terrestrials, yes—and once, in the era or our greatness, it was so with Nrlanians. We, too, were once well balanced with our sub-material interlocked energy-mass fields. But then—someone built the first *sarniall*—which is an ether warp, but on a titanic scale.

"There must have been some sort of explosion of energy controlling the warp generator, because it not only rocked the planet by upsetting its sub-material balance, that is, in the finer interlocked matter called ether, but it simultaneously swept our inner essence out of the total flesh of the race."

Shahn gaped. "We lost our souls…"

Vrulnus winced. "There is a strange intellectual revulsion to that term, in English, since it has been so long associated with mysticism and philosophical alchemy. Let us, instead, use the ancient and little known Nrlanian equivalent, *karn,* which means the counterpart of gross material flesh in sub-material form—the interlocked counter-balance of our carnate selves. So I may answer you: yes—the total *karn* of the race was dislodged but not lost."

"*Not* lost." Shahn's eyes shone with an insuppressible light of hope.

"Before we go into that," said Vrulnus, "I must explain to you this fact: That Nature always seeks a balance. Shorn of this balance between gross matter and sub-matter—that is, between flesh and *karn*—by processes incomprehensible to myself, a natural method of regenerating the *karn* evolved, unknown to us. The result was a negative thing—the mutation."

"Metamorphosis!"

"Yes—our curse. And the antidote—"

"Would be to replace the original *karn.*"

"Correct again. And now you see—after witnessing the faith of Earthmen in their own duality—I became encouraged to re-examine my hitherto bizarre hypothesis as to what had happened to us. I think that catastrophic ether warp of ancient times did not destroy our collective *karn.* I believe that it eddied outward on the periphery of that warp, and settled on Gral."

"Ao!" exclaimed Shahn.

"Concept incredible," said Vrulnus, "but perhaps true. A single *karn,* representing our lost race and our lost greatness. An eternal thing, waiting to fill the void of our flesh and wash us clean of the curse of mutation."

Shahn leapt to his feet and paced the deck, his face bathed in perspiration. Now Lillian knew the magnitude of Vrulnus' mind. The concept was yet beyond her grasp.

"I cannot consciously understand quite all that you seek to convey," she told Vrulnus. "But on the fringe of the subconscious I feel what you mean. I almost wonder if we're sane."

Shahn turned about. "But even so," he said, swiftly, "what if it was true? What if Ao is the lost, total soul of the race. How do we—"

"There was one difficulty that bothered me," said Vrulnus. "But now it seems that some force of predestination has thrown this lovely woman into a predicament analogous to yours, Shahn. The *sarniall* dislodged her *karn.* She is, as you are, unbalanced, and thus carries the seed of mutation—"

Lillian opened her eyes wide. She tried not to scream. Shahn looked at her, astounded at the concept that she, too, might become a Metamorph.

"But that may all be avoided—" Vrulnus started to say.

IN THAT moment, they were all thrown to the floor as the star ship automatically swerved on its course.

"Meteors" shouted Vrulnus. "Lillian, get into a bunk. Shahn, strap her in. The course alternator is designed for *us,* not her."

Lillian was aware of Shahn swaying over her in the shock of rapid course changes, while he strapped her down. Then oblivion settled upon her. She did not know that she slept for years, after that, because when the meteors passed Vrulnus put her into suspended animation for the great crossing over the star roads to the distant grave of Nrlan.

After Shahn had submitted to the treatment also, he was not aware of an occurrence, which would have shattered, utterly, his awakening dream of life.

For as Vrulnus lay down on a hiberbunk preparatory to giving himself the needle that would place his life forces in prolonged suspension, he suddenly stopped, looking in amazement at his hands. His gray eyes widened slowly, then his powerful face contorted in fear and anguish.

"No," he groaned aloud. *"No!"*

But the evidence of his senses was incontrovertible.

Out there in the far reaches of interstellar space, in the confines of the hurtling star ship, while his precious companions slept in the helpless sleep of years, Vrulnus' mighty hands were slowly excreting a greenish slime—which would increase and harden, all over his body.

It might take ten years, this mutation, but in the end—at the end of their vital journey to Ao—he would be the virtual Khal of every Metamorph that had yet evolved.

And when the process was complete, he would be *hungry.* But Shahn and Lillian were unaware of this. They slept blissfully at his side.

CHAPTER THIRTEEN
Battle of the Khals

BENEATH the shell of consciousness, dreams and memory combined in Shahn's struggling mind. After ten long years, he was stirring out of suspended animation.

*   *   *

Nrlan!

Graveless is Nrlan, world of the dead great past. It drifts a nebulous cold cloud of death and ashes down the shoreless sea—emptiness where once were dreams and love and laughter—and dark despair.

Beloved mate, wearer of my own scar of *san,* Sralna, she of the summer moons—

But no!

He stood on a cliff overlooking a strange sea on another world, watching the figure of a girl hurtle to her death—so beautiful she had been, so young.

And then—a pair of clear blue eyes, raven hair, a slim-waisted girl who washed dishes in a sink.

"No," he muttered, groaning aloud.

Too late did he stagger to his feet to grapple with the bullet-torn man who held in his dying hands the glowing *sarniall,* its terrible forces concentrated upon the girl. Darkness, like a negative entity, swirled about Lillian Hammer, and she paled—

Swirling shadows, like mists of night, rose up from the motionless chrysalides. They seemed to dance in a slow rhythm, like nameless monsters out of the unvisited pits of delirium.

Then Vrulnus raised the *sarniall* and fired. Young women, naked and beautiful, held out innocent babes—but he fired remorselessly.

It was over now. Vrulnus had saved their dream of life. And Ao waited at the end of the journey…

*   *   *

"Vrulnus," he cried, sitting up suddenly and looking about him in the crypt-like ship.

Instead of Vrulnus, he saw on the hiberbunk beside him the beautiful, sleeping form of the Earthwoman—Lillian, barred from his life by obstacles insurmountable; bound to him eternally for the same reason. He loved her. She was the *karn* of his lonely flesh.

"Thank Ao," he exclaimed. "She lives."

And then—then only did he turn to look for Vrulnus—his mighty mentor and saviour of worlds—most precious man—

With the mercurial swiftness of his kind, Shahn tensed so strenuously that the tendons and veins of his body sprang into ghastly relief upon his flesh, contorting his face. After a full minute of numbing shock, Shahn emitted a hoarse shriek of mortal anguish.

And Lillian awoke, to gaze upon what had once been Vrulnus, *Khal* of Nrlan.

HOURS passed before Shahn finally yielded to the conviction that Lillian's mind was gone. The shock had been too great. He locked her in the observation dome, where she mumbled incoherently at the unfamiliar stars of these distant depths of the void.

Then he turned himself resolutely to the task of disposing of the grotesque chrysalide that had once been the greatest human alive—grotesque, it was, because of its weird lack of symmetry. One leg was missing, and on the floor lay an artificial limb.

Heart-breaking as it was, in his tragic new loneliness, to dump the inhuman shell of what had once been his beloved teacher out of the airlock, he set himself to the task. He began to unloosen the half-parted straps of the swollen, glistening thing.

The ship darkened ominously.

He paused, suddenly overtaken by an olden fear—a recollection of the cloying death-grip of the Metamorph.

It lived. Its shell was here in his hands—but its great negative essence surrounded him.

"Vrulnus," he cried out at the condensing shadows, shivering in the strange, intolerable coldness that was of the mind rather than of the flesh. "Vrulnus—this is Shahn. You can't..." He leapt to an opposite extremity of the deck and looked back.

On top of the chrysalide sat the opaque shadow of a man. As he had been powerful and incomparable among humans, now Vrulnus' antithesis was the undeniable dark *Khal* of Metamorphs—the master evil force that was capable of extending the influence of his kind throughout the universe.

Had Shahn been of Earth, or an ordinary Nrlanian, he might have succumbed totally to his instinctive fear. But in him flowed the blood of the *Khals*. Slowly, he collected himself, and a fire of wrath lighted in his dark eyes.

"It cannot be," he said.

"But it is," said the shadow-man, in ghostly tones. "Just as your mind has told you, it is so. This is my ship, Shahn, and you are my pilot. I shall return now—to Earth. And there..."

"No," retorted Shahn. "No—there must be another way. Look, we are opposite poles. I am now the human *Khal*..."

"And I the inhuman *Khal*. Our purposes are diametrically opposed, Shahn."

"Exactly. Therefore, we are two *Khals*—met between two opposed camps—to come to terms."

"*My* terms, Shahn."

"No—*mutual* terms."

"This presupposes that you have something to offer—something to bargain *with*. And you have not."

Shahn's nostrils flared. "Only an interesting challenge, Vrulnus," he retorted, between his teeth.

"That presupposes again," said the shadow, "that we are atavisms subject to emotion. The appeal of a challenge lies in the glandular emotion of pride. We have none. No, Shahn—offer me no battle of empires. My wants are quite simple. In fact—I might offer you some recourse, in return for—"

The shadowy figure seemed to be concentrating on the closed observation dome, where Lillian was imprisoned.

"Simply stated," said the man-shadow. "I am *hungry.*"

Shahn felt his flesh quiver. A coldness in his bones dampened his temper. He paused, breathlessly, thinking fast. This was another one of those fateful hinges of decision whereon swung the gate of destiny. If he could not gain the upper hand on this thing now—

"How am I to give that which you can take?" he asked, cautiously. "You'd better crawl into your shell and hibernate. It's a long journey back, Vrulnus. You will get hungry again, you know."

Already, the dark shadow had begun to attenuate, its now amorphous presence drifting toward the door of the observation chamber.

"And then you will want *me*," Shahn continued swiftly. "But I am your pilot. Without me, the ship cannot reach your goal."

He waited, tensing, until the shadowy mist had seeped under the door of the chamber where Lillian sat incarcerated. Then, in an almost invisible flash of motion, he pounced on Vrulnus' forgotten artificial limb. Couched within its upper framework was the shield generator, still powered by the permanent Nrlanian battery with which its inventor had supplied it.

Instantly, the living chrysalide warned its projection, and the shadow returned into the room as if blown by an etheric wind. It loomed, mantis-like, above him, but in that moment the shield sprang into lambent life, surrounding Shahn with its welcome canopy of energy.

The great shadow hovered over the bowl of energy, not touching it, but blocking out light. Only dimly could Shahn see the gleaming chrysalide at his side, by the light of the glowing tubes in the generator he held.

Vaguely, as from an infinite distance, a menacing thought crept into his mind:

I'll reach you, Shahn, eventually, through the gross molecular structure of the deck. Don't force me to destroy you. You will one day take my place, Shahn—as the Khal of Metamorphs.

"No," shouted Shahn. "Never!" He pulled at the chrysalide, crashing it to the deck. Placing the field generator on top of it, he pushed it toward the airlock.

That will avail you nothing, Shahn, came the distant, feeble thought of the projection beyond the shield. *You have yet to learn of my powers. I warn you...*

Relentlessly, Shahn kept at his task. He opened the inner hatch, and pushed the living black shell inside the lock. After snatching up the artificial limb that housed the generator, he drew back, closed the hatch, then depressed the stud controlling the outer hatch. And still the persistent shadow hovered over him.

He ran to the control room, followed instantly by the evil darkness.

Fool! came the distant thought. *I am of the ether. I can distort your magnetics—alter your course!*

"Try it," shouted Shahn, as he lay the generator on the panel and raced his hands over the console. Meanwhile, he prayed to Ao for Lillian's salvation, as he jerked the star ship off course, dipped it viciously, and dumped the chrysalide out of the open lock. Then he accelerated.

The shadow of Vrulnus dissolved.

Shahn cut the force generator, thankful for the return of the lights. He rushed to the observation chamber, to find Lillian unconscious on the floor, bleeding from her nose and mouth. With a barely audible cry of anguish, he picked her up in his arms and took her to a hiberbunk, where he strapped her in. Her breasts rose and fell in fitful breathing,

The star ship swayed almost imperceptibly then braked its headlong plunge through emptiness. He dashed back to the controls, not daring to believe the Metamorph could actually affect the propelling forces of the vessel.

Yet the instruments told him that some strange new phenomenon was impeding the star drive. He swore, pouring in more power, trying to shake off the cloying drag—and at last he felt a clear, clean surge of flight, as though the ship, like a frightened lark, had eluded the talons of a hawk.

Suddenly, darkness rushed upon him, and the cold of the outer void paralyzed his limbs. In spite of the chrysalide's distance, its projection still reached him.

With mind-staggering power, Vrulnus' angered death-thoughts pierced his consciousness like a mighty scythe: *Pick me up, Shahn, or die!*

Shahn remembered—he was his teacher's disciple, and the teacher was reaching at him over a terrible gulf of distance. He braced his mind, blocking in the shield he had been taught to build against alien penetration. Slowly, the chill abated, but the shadow yet clung to him, trying now to drain the electric elixir of life from his body. Nausea swept upon him. He sweated, blocked, fought—and *moved*.

Slowly, in the midst of the grimmest struggle of his life, he turned to the panel, pushing in the acceleration stud, increasing the distance between shadow and shell by tens of thousands of miles.

Then—like a bubble—the shadow broke into a withering mist and was gone. Shahn sagged weakly until his knees crumpled under him. He sat on the floor, leaning against the panel cabinet, eyes staring into nothingness…

CHAPTER FOURTEEN
Ao—and the Dream of Life

DAYS of deceleration followed, Shahn's instruments told him he was nearing the old system of Nrlan, and already the great double sun, which had warmed his incubator, centuries past, had become visible to the unaided eye.

But great Nrlan was now only a vast, eccentric ring of asteroids—and somewhere among those haunted fragments swung dark Gral, the moon of Ao, his mysterious goal. By terrestrial standards, Gral was a planet, he remembered, being some four thousand miles in diameter and possessing an atmosphere. For all he knew, it might even be inhabited by some unknown form of life.

As Lillian convalesced slowly from her physical impairment resulting from the ship's undue acceleration during the battle with Vrulnus, Shahn looked moodily ahead at the ever-expanding Nrlanian system—and wondered just what he was supposed to do when he arrived on the moon of Ao. The final mystery of the ages was to have been revealed to him by his great teacher. Vrulnus knew the final answer, but now he was gone forever. It devolved upon him alone to solve the enigma.

Whenever he would stand over Lillian where she lay on the hiberbunk, he would ponder on one of Vrulnus' last, cryptic statements: "There was one difficulty that bothered me; but now it seems that some force of predestination has thrown this lovely woman into a predicament analogous to yours, Shahn."

What did it mean? The analogous predicament referred to their emptiness, to the absence of their *karns*. Why should the fact that she, too, was thus afflicted solve a difficulty with relation to Ao?

He did not know.

*   *   *

GRAL'S dark side lay beneath the star ship. The ghostly halo of atmosphere floated like an ethereal shim above shadowed ravines and mountains touched with starlight. Deep within one far distant gorge, in the midst of abysmal night, gleamed a bright, shimmering light, like a shackled god of a lost dawn—imprisoned, gigantic, chained, waiting through eternity to be unleashed.

As Shahn looked upon this flaming aura of light energy in his telescope—like some vast nebula of creative world fire lost in the void—he was afflicted with a form of ague. He trembled with the presentiment of Ao's *living presence*. It offended his *Khal's* blood to fear—yet he feared this awesome, waiting entity.

Lillian stood beside him, afflicted with partial amnesia. She only remembered him, but of Vrulnus or Ao she recalled nothing. Nor was she aware that she had ever been the victim of a *sarniall*.

"What is it?" she asked him, innocently.

He took hold of her hand and searched her eyes. "I don't know," he told her. "But we must go there."

"Why, Shahn? Is that home?"

"Perhaps—or maybe not a location, exactly. It is more related to time, dear."

"Time? What do you mean?"

"Perhaps—it is Tomorrow. There was once a dream of life—a dream that a great teacher of mine once described to me alone. This may be the secret of that dream. Shall we go?"

Childlike, Lillian clapped her hands together. "Oh, let's go see what it is!"

Shahn led her out of the observation chamber and into the control room. The girl wondered at his hand in hers, for it seemed to tremble.

THEY wore heated suits and air helmets against the cold of Gral. He led her carefully over the dark, virgin terrain of the satellite, up the high-walled gorge toward the soaring aurora that loomed above Ao's abode.

In Shahn's eyes grew a light of wonder, of uncomprehended hope. In his blood tingled an unvoiced message. His face was alight with the growing illumination of the entity awaiting him.

As he walked thus, Lillian caught his mood and responded equally to the ecstatic experience of revelation. She needed no guidance now. Her footsteps quickened over the volcanic ground, and at last it was she who guided him.

In the midst of ecstasy, awe and wonder engendered Shahn's previous unknown fear. Instinctively, he slowed his pace, yearning to go on into that world of light, yet dreading the shock of virtual resurrection. For was not his empty human shell to be filled with the eternal essence? What would it be like to bear within him the conglomerate *soul of a race?*

He would no longer be himself.

"No, Lillian—stop," he cried, halting.

But the girl would not be stayed. She left him standing there. Entranced, she continued onward.

And then, at last, he knew the meaning of Vrulnus' cryptic remarks about her. The difficulty with Ao was that, as the macro-*karn* of the ancient master race of Nrlan, it possessed both male and female components. Or could this difference in gender be applied to such as Ao? If so, then a physical male *plus* a female was necessary for the impending mystical phenomenon. He, therefore, was also a vital necessity for Ao's long awaited dual incarnation.

"Wait," he cried.

But before he could proceed, the magnificent aurora darkened in his eyes, and he felt the chill hand of death upon him.

So near, Shahn, came a dark thought into his mind, *and yet so far.*

"Vrulnus," he yelled, already struggling to block his mind against the enveloping darkness of the Metamorph. "How did you—"

How did my chrysalide become a satellite of Gral? My secret, Shahn, which you will never know.

"But let me go on. I must join her!"

No. She may embrace the Essence, but to no avail, for she will be stranded. You are my pilot, Shahn. We are returning to Earth. Submit, or die.

"And you with me," he shouted, his body bathed in sweat from his mental exertions.

The darkness and the coldness waned momentarily as he blocked his mind fiercely and struggled forward, up the gorge. Then he stumbled and fell as the darkness returned. His senses reeled.

*   *   *

HOW long he lay there he could not know. When he opened his eyes it was to witness a sight beyond human experience.

Between himself and the light of Ao, now strangely diminished to half its former intensity, he saw the hovering shadow. It densified angrily and rushed up the gorge toward a human figure that advanced to meet it.

"Lillian," he cried out in alarm, rising to his feet. And then he paused, incapacitated.

In the comparative darkness of the gorge at this point, her form was limned with a mysterious light. Her beautiful face seemed virtually to glow. She moved confidently to meet the Metamorph.

Vrulnus swooped down upon her, trying to envelop her in darkness. But that was the dark *Khal's* last move. Suddenly, the darkness fell away like tempest-scattered dust, and was no more.

Beaming upon him, Lillian now approached and reached out her hand to Shahn.

"Vrulnus," came her vital, ringing voice through the phones, "is but a living shell without a *karn*. Helpless, untenanted by his negative essence, he will swing through the lonely courses of the void forever. Come, Shahn. Here is your dream of life."

And she led him into the waiting aura, where light alone was vision, and titanic life flooded him with sight and sense unmeasured...

SHAHN and Lillian stood together before the star ship, looking back on the darkened gorge. Gone was Ao, for it had been reborn. In them resided the macro-*karn* of the ancient race.

"We *are* no more," said Shahn.

She smiled. "Not as we were—"

"Our like is unparalleled in existence."

"This is spiritual mutation."

"Perhaps it is symbolic of Man's next change."

"Earth awaits our return, Shahn."

"No. First, the great dream must be born. When that is accomplished—then we may return to rescue Earth.

The shining woman smiled upon him.

"What *is* your great dream of life, Shahn?"

The shining man took her hand in his, turning toward the ship.

"Come," he said. "We will build it."

THE END

If you've enjoyed this book, you will not want to miss these terrific titles…

ARMCHAIR SCI-FI & HORROR DOUBLE NOVELS, $12.95 each

D-21   **EMPIRE OF EVIL** by Robert Arnette
THE SIGN OF THE TIGER by Alan E. Nourse & J. A. Meyer

D-22   **OPERATION SQUARE PEG** by Frank Belknap Long
ENCHANTRESS OF VENUS by Leigh Brackett

D-23   **THE LIFE WATCH** by Lester del Rey
CREATURES OF THE ABYSS by Murray Leinster

D-24   **LEGION OF LAZARUS** by Edmond Hamilton
STAR HUNTER by Andre Norton

D-25   **EMPIRE OF WOMEN** by John Fletcher
ONE OF OUR CITIES IS MISSING by Irving Cox

D-26   **THE WRONG SIDE OF PARADISE** by Raymond F. Jones
THE INVOLUNTARY IMMORTALS by Rog Phillips

D-27   **EARTH QUARTER** by Damon Knight
ENVOY TO NEW WORLDS by Keith Laumer

D-28   **SLAVES TO THE METAL HORDE** by Milton Lesser
HUNTERS OUT OF TIME by Joseph E. Kelleam

D-29   **RX JUPITER SAVE US** by Ward Moore
BEWARE THE USURPERS by Geoff St. Reynard

D-30   **SECRET OF THE SERPENT** by Don Wilcox
CRUSADE ACROSS THE VOID by Dwight V. Swain

ARMCHAIR SCIENCE FICTION CLASSICS, $12.95 each

C-7   **THE SHAVER MYSTERY, Book One**
by Richard S. Shaver

C-8   **THE SHAVER MYSTERY, Book Two**
by Richard S. Shaver

C-9   **MURDER IN SPACE**
by David V. Reed

ARMCHAIR MASTERS OF SCIENCE FICTION SERIES, $16.95 each

M-3   **MASTERS OF SCIENCE FICTION, Vol. Three**
Robert Sheckley, "The Perfect Woman" and other tales

M-4   **MASTERS OF SCIENCE FICTION, Vol. Four**
Mack Reynolds, Part One, "Stowaway" and other tales

If you've enjoyed this book, you will not want to miss these terrific titles…

ARMCHAIR SCI-FI & HORROR DOUBLE NOVELS, $12.95 each

D-31   **A HOAX IN TIME** by Keith Laumer
INSIDE EARTH by Poul Anderson

D-32   **TERROR STATION** by Dwight V. Swain
THE WEAPON FROM ETERNITY by Dwight V. Swain

D-33   **THE SHIP FROM INFINITY** by Edmond Hamilton
TAKEOFF by C. M. Kornbluth

D-34   **THE METAL DOOM** by David H. Keller
TWELVE TIMES ZERO by Howard Browne

D-35   **HUNTERS OUT OF SPACE** by Joseph Kelleam
INVASION FROM THE DEEP by Paul W. Fairman,

D-36   **THE BEES OF DEATH** by Robert Moore Williams
A PLAGUE OF PYTHONS by Frederik Pohl

D-37   **THE LORDS OF QUARMALL** by Fritz Leiber and Harry Fischer
BEACON TO ELSEWHERE by James H. Schmitz

D-38   **BEYOND PLUTO** by John S. Campbell
ARTERY OF FIRE by Thomas N. Scortia

D-39   **SPECIAL DELIVERY** by Kris Neville
NO TIME FOR TOFFEE by Charles F. Meyers

D-40   **JUNGLE IN THE SKY** by Milton Lesser
RECALLED TO LIFE by Robert Silverberg

ARMCHAIR SCIENCE FICTION CLASSICS, $12.95 each

C-10   **MARS IS MY DESTINATION**
by Frank Belknap Long

C-11   **SPACE PLAGUE**
by George O. Smith

C-12   **SO SHALL YE REAP**
by Rog Phillips

ARMCHAIR SCI-FI & HORROR GEMS SERIES, $12.95 each

G-3   **SCIENCE FICTION GEMS, Vol. Two**
James Blish and others

G-4   **HORROR GEMS, Vol. Two**
Joseph Payne Brennan and others

If you've enjoyed this book, you will not want to miss these terrific titles…

ARMCHAIR SCI-FI & HORROR DOUBLE NOVELS, $12.95 each

D-41 **FULL CYCLE** by Clifford D. Simak
IT WAS THE DAY OF THE ROBOT by Frank Belknap Long

D-42 **THIS CROWDED EARTH** by Robert Bloch
REIGN OF THE TELEPUPPETS by Daniel Galouye

D-43 **THE CRISPIN AFFAIR** by Jack Sharkey
THE RED HELL OF JUPITER by Paul Ernst

D-44 **PLANET OF DREAD** by Dwight V. Swain
WE THE MACHINE by Gerald Vance

D-45 **THE STAR HUNTER** by Edmond Hamilton
THE ALIEN by Raymond F. Jones

D-46 **WORLD OF IF** by Rog Phillips
SLAVE RAIDERS FROM MERCURY by Don Wilcox

D-47 **THE ULTIMATE PERIL** by Robert Abernathy
PLANET OF SHAME by Bruce Elliot

D-48 **THE FLYING EYES** by J. Hunter Holly
SOME FABULOUS YONDER by Phillip Jose Farmer

D-49 **THE COSMIC BUNGLERS** by Geoff St. Reynard
THE BUTTONED SKY by Geoff St. Reynard

D-50 **TYRANTS OF TIME** by Milton Lesser
PARIAH PLANET by Murray Leinster

ARMCHAIR SCIENCE FICTION CLASSICS, $12.95 each

C-13 **SUNKEN WORLD**
by Stanton A. Coblentz

C-14 **THE LAST VIAL**
by Sam McClatchie, M. D.

C-15 **WE WHO SURVIVED (THE FIFTH ICE AGE)**
by Sterling Noel

ARMCHAIR MASTERS OF SCIENCE FICTION SERIES, $16.95 each

MS-5 **MASTERS OF SCIENCE FICTION, Vol. Five**
Winston K. Marks—Test Colony and other tales

MS-6 **MASTERS OF SCIENCE FICTION, Vol. Six**
Fritz Leiber—Deadly Moon and other tales

If you've enjoyed this book, you will not want to miss these terrific titles…

ARMCHAIR SCI-FI & HORROR DOUBLE NOVELS, $12.95 each

D-101 **THE CONQUEST OF THE PLANETS** by John W. Campbell
THE MAN WHO ANNEXED THE MOON by Bob Olsen

D-102 **WEAPON FROM THE STARS** by Rog Phillips
THE EARTH WAR by Mack Reynolds

D-103 **THE ALIEN INTELLIGENCE** by Jack Williamson
INTO THE FOURTH DIMENSION by Ray Cummings

D-104 **THE CRYSTAL PLANETOIDS** by Stanton A. Coblentz
SURVIVORS FROM 9,000 B. C. by Robert Moore Williams

D-105 **THE TIME PROJECTOR** by David H. Keller, M.D. and David Lasser
STRANGE COMPULSION by Philip Jose Farmer

D-106 **WHOM THE GODS WOULD SLAY** by Paul W. Fairman
MEN IN THE WALLS by William Tenn

D-107 **LOCKED WORLDS** by Edmond Hamilton
THE LAND THAT TIME FORGOT by Edgar Rice Burroughs

D-108 **STAY OUT OF SPACE** by Dwight V. Swain
REBELS OF THE RED PLANET by Charles L. Fontenay

D-109 **THE METAMORPHS** by S. J. Byrne
MICROCOSMIC BUCCANEERS by Harl Vincent

D-110 **YOU CAN'T ESCAPE FROM MARS** by E. K. Jarvis
THE MAN WITH FIVE LIVES by David V. Reed

ARMCHAIR SCIENCE FICTION CLASSICS, $12.95 each

C-34 **30 DAY WONDER**
by Richard Wilson

C-35 **G.O.G. 666**
by John Taine

C-36 **RALPH 124C 41+**
by Hugo Gernsback

ARMCHAIR SCI-FI & HORROR GEMS SERIES, $12.95 each

G-11 **SCIENCE FICTION GEMS, Vol. Six**
Edmond Hamilton and others

G-12 **HORROR GEMS, Vol. Six**
H. P. Lovecraft and others

AN INVASION OF ATOM-SIZED SPACE PIRATES!

Young Grayson worshipped his mentor, the master scientist known as Minott V8CA. Under his tutelage Grayson had become well versed in many forms of science and advanced scientific theory. But Minott had discovered something so incredible, so startling, that it was nearly beyond Grayson's comprehension to understand it. Minott had uncovered the existence of a new universe—a universe teaming with new worlds, new stars, and most importantly…new life! However, this vast sea of seemingly endless space was different than anything previously known to man, because its entirety was smaller than the tiniest of molecules—a mere electron orbiting some unknown atom. But within this infinitesimally small realm, laying in wait, was a deadly alien force—the Prags, whose sole purpose was to conquer all new worlds—and their next target was Earth itself!

CAST OF CHARACTERS

GRAYSON
He was the loyal apprentice to a master scientist—and this loyalty would soon thrust him into an incredible adventure.

MINOTT
He was a brilliant scientist, but a slight miscalculation and his own lack of courage helped put the Earth in grave danger.

LOLA
Her skin was smooth and she had perfect features to go along with the most wondrous pair of eyes Grayson had ever seen.

THE GREAT ONES
They were mere brains with huge, semi-transparent heads, immense eyes, and bodies shrunken beyond all belief.

THE KAMA
This ruthless Prag space commander was shocked to find that two of his Elsian captives were beings from another universe.

ORIL
He was a prisoner of the Prags, but he was dedicated to a plan that would see the end of their tyrannical ways.

ATAR
He was a strong, proud Elsian and Lola's father, but he shrank in horror when he discovered she was to be sacrificed to the Prags.

MICROCOSMIC BUCCANEERS

By
HARL VINCENT

ARMCHAIR FICTION
PO Box 4369, Medford, Oregon 97504

*For more information about Armchair Books and products, visit our
website at…*

www.armchairfiction.com

Or email us at…

armchairfiction@yahoo.com

CHAPTER ONE
An Astounding Discovery

IT was utterly incomprehensible, yet it was true. They had seen it with their own eyes. Young Grayson R36B stared at his father's friend with amazement written large on his lean, bronze countenance. Minott V8CA, Director of Physical Research of the eighth Terrestrial district, returned the stare with something of awe in his tired gray eyes.

"Grayson, my boy," he said, "we have succeeded beyond my most optimistic hopes. We have delved into the secrets of the microcosmos. We have located one of its innumerable universes and have there found an inconceivably minute world with its own sun, moon and stars, and peopled by living, thinking creatures who resemble the white race of our earth in physical appearance. It is quite unthinkable, but here is the evidence."

He glanced again into the eyepiece of the massive instrument before which they stood.

"I still cannot understand it," remarked the younger man, slowly and with a perplexed frown. "Of course I'm as yet ignorant of all excepting the mere rudiments of science. But it seems to me I have read, or perhaps you told me, that these electrons, of which our infinitesimal world is one, are traveling at great speed even in matter of considerable density. How, then, can your super-microscope view these objects as if they were stationary?"

"That is a feature I neglected to mention. The initial magnification, as I believe I told you, is accomplished by a powerful ray of vibrations. This ray impinges on the object to be viewed and is the first stage of magnification in the system, which gives us such enormous powers. The ray, in addition to giving us the first ten thousand diameters, has the property of following the motions of which you speak. Its far end oscillates in exact harmony with the motions of molecule or atom or electron as the case may be, while the source of the ray remains stationary and thus impresses a stationary image on the object reflector to the second stage of the instrument."

Grayson R36B nodded in comprehension, though he was unable to picture in his mind's eye such movements of a ray so small as to be unmeasurable and, in fact, invisible in a high power microscope of standard type. This was but one of the many things he had yet to learn. But he found the mysteries of science intensely interesting as propounded by his mentor, and he looked forward happily to many years of such association with the great man into whose care he had been legally placed at the death of his father, two years ago.

"What is the next step?" he asked.

Minott V8CA pondered the question. He had been wondering over the same subject. He was not satisfied with knowing as little as they had been able to see of the inhabitants of the tiny world now visible in the eyepiece of his instrument. He wanted to view them from still closer, to learn more of their lives and of their history. He replied, half-jesting, "I should like to pay them a visit."

"Pay them a visit? But that is impossible."

"Nothing is impossible. We are living in the thirty-third century, my boy. Fifteen centuries ago it was thought impossible that man would ever fly—mind you, fly in the atmosphere like a bird. Ten centuries ago it was thought that gravity could never be counteracted or overcome. And less than five centuries ago a trip to one of the planets was held to be the height of ridiculous imagination. Yet all of these things have been accomplished, and much more. No, I would not say the trip is impossible."

"But it's hardly probable, is it?"

"Hardly. Though the thing merits consideration."

The great scientist mused further. His young protégé let his mind dwell upon the bizarre possibility suggested by the older man. There was no more adventure in the world, he ruminated. Some of the ancient sound films that had been used as a part of his education portrayed stirring events of the distant past. Adventures had been commonplace in those heroic days—ocean flights in tiny, wind-buffeted vessels that looked as though they would never weather the storms—struggles of man against the wilderness, building huge dams across turbulent rivers or erecting strange steel towers, that carried power lines through well-nigh impenetrable jungles. Wars and rebellions in remote provinces had likewise appealed to him. But in his own day there was none of that, none of the excitement that had been the lot of adventurous youth in the dark ages. There were no storms now to buffet the gigantic airliners crossing the oceans, for science had conquered the weather. There was no wilderness or jungle. Nor were there remote provinces, where battles might be fought and deeds of valor might be performed. The world was entirely civilized and overpopulated. Several generations back it had been considered somewhat of an adventure to make a trip to Mars or to Venus, but even this no longer provided excitement, for these planets were now but a few hours away and were so like Earth in civilization and appearance as to present no novelty for a visiting terrestrial. Now here was a new possibility in the microcosmos—and who knew how many more of the tiny worlds might be inhabited? But he could not bring himself to seriously consider the probability of ever reaching one of them.

"Grayson," spoke the older man, interrupting his line of thought, "I intend to do some heavy thinking over this thing. You know the control of our physical size is a comparatively simple matter now, within limits. Of course we have standardized on six feet three inches as man's stature and five feet eleven as woman's, but there is no reason this might not be altered greatly if desired. By the use of one of the hormones of the pituitary gland we might grow giants of eight feet stature and by causing certain endocrine deficiencies it is possible to dwarf a man to a fourth of normal height. By similar processes it might be that we could contrive to reduce ourselves to the dimensions necessary for life on our newly found electron world."

"You really think something might be done?"

" 'Might be' is the proper term. It's far from being a simple matter. But, as I said before, I shall think about it seriously."

"Supposing it were possible to reduce our bodies to the proper size. We should then be the distance of many universes from that grain of sand, which contains our Lilliputian world. We might as well be at the outermost edge of our own galactic* universe. How would we ever reach it?"

"That is probably the most difficult part of the problem, and the one requiring the most thought. But it must be susceptible to solution, if not in our lifetime at least at some future date."

Grayson's delight at the words of his guardian was evident in his eyes and it abated but little at the further warning that all this talk of visiting the populated electron was extremely fanciful. And that night he dreamed of green forests and of running streams and of all those things that had existed for him only in history and in carefully preserved picturings. For Grayson R36B was not yet twenty-five years of age.

----

* Galactic: indicates the Milky Way as the location of a cosmic or astronomical system. It means "milky" (from the Greek).

CHAPTER TWO
By Means of the Fourth Dimension

WITH the passing of four months the scientist found himself little closer to the solution of the problem than when it was first presented. Experiments with white mice as subjects had progressed to the point where these lively creatures had been reduced to the size of blood corpuscles, a dozen or more of them scampering about in an opening the size of a pin point indented in a thin paraffin coating on a microscope slide. They were still far from their goal and the young man, who had assisted with all the work, was on the point of despairing entirely.

Then there came the day when Grayson R36B was startled from his observation of the electron world through the super-microscope, by an ecstatic shout from his guardian.

"What is it?" he asked excitedly.

"We've been working on an entirely wrong basis, Grayson. But now I see the light. The fourth dimension!"

"Fourth dimension?" repeated his ward, blankly.

"Certainly, I don't know why I haven't thought of it before. We'll visit the tiny planet by its agency."

"But—but I thought that the fourth dimension was only a mathematical conception—that there was no real knowledge of it."

"You are quite right, my boy, as far as any published data is concerned. But there have been experiments—- successful ones too—that were apparently of no practical use. Now we have the practical use. You understand, of course, that even though you do not perceive a fourth dimension, all objects in our universe must be possessed of this abstruse quality in order to exist. We live and breathe in a four-dimensional world that is part of a four-dimensional universe. The so-called dimension has been variously explained but for our purpose we need not enter into any of the various arguments that have been brought up. It is not time in the strict sense that we are interested in, but the time-space relationship, and it is that relationship I intend to employ in entering that little world at which you have been gazing."

"You mean, if the time-space relationship as applied to our physical existence is altered, we shall then have no difficulty in making the journey?"

"That is it exactly, my boy, we as human beings are four-dimensional entities peculiarly adapted to life in our own environment. These entities occupy space in a definite volume we are pleased to designate by three dimensions. But the interval, the time-space relationship, is what makes us as we are. Size is only relative and if everything in the universe was suddenly to become a million times larger or a million times smaller, we should not be aware of the difference, for our standards of measurement would also have altered in like proportion,"

"But how to effect such a change?"

"I'm coming to that. There is a plane, which in 3281 was designated by Rollin D4Y as the hyperphysical plane. And Rollin experimented at considerable length in rotating objects in and out of this plane by various methods. In the most successful of the methods used, a purely mechanical means, he found it possible to rotate living creatures instantaneously into and out of the hyperphysical existence without harm. By instantaneous, I mean that the transition must take place within the period of not more than two or three heartbeats of the subject. We shall go further than did Rollin. We shall not only enter the hyperphysical plane, but shall project ourselves into the delectable world of the microcosmos and there emerge as entities adaptable to the greatly different existence."

Grayson's eyes popped. "You think it can be done?" he gasped.

"I'm sure of it. And quite simply too."

Minott hurried to a large cupboard at the side of the laboratory and there brought to view a dust-covered apparatus that Grayson had never seen. This was provided with a box-like base set on four casters, and it was trundled forth by the excited scientist.

"A duplicate of Rollin's apparatus," he explained, busying himself with a duster.

GRAYSON watched with intense interest as the older man uncovered the upper portion of the mechanism. There was a huge vacuum tube, one of the largest he had ever seen, and about this there clustered a maze of helices of tiny silver ribbon. "Two arms swung out from the side of the box, and each of these carried what appeared to be a parabolic reflector, also of silver. There was a heavy cable to which a wall plug was attached, and Minott connected this with a base receptacle nearby. He withdrew a slide from the side of the box and arranged the two reflectors to focus on the slide. Then he reached for one of the small cages containing a normal white mouse and this he placed on the slide. With all arranged to his satisfaction, he pulled a switch at the side of the mechanism. There came a roar from within and the great vacuum tube lighted to a dull red glow. The mouse scampered unconcerned in its cage.

"Now, observe closely," said Minott, placing his finger on a small button that Grayson had not noticed.

He pressed the button and the universe seemed to totter. The very space about them seemed to warp and twist. The lively creature in the little cage vanished as suddenly and utterly as if a genie had whisked it away, Grayson stared dumbfounded. A second passed. Two seconds. Then, in a puff of blue haze, the mouse once more nosed about in its coop. The accompanying wrench of the space in which they stood left Grayson trembling and aghast.

"Good grief!" he exclaimed. "There's strong medicine in that box all right! So that's the way we are going?"

Yes. Excepting we must combine Rollin's apparatus with my super-microscope."

"Combine it?"

"Of course. Otherwise we should not reach our destination; we would merely return to our normal existence, as did our little subject. With our existence transferred to the hyperphysical plane, we'll be whisked along the minute ray of the super-microscope, which is now trained on the place we are to visit. In reentering the purely physical plane, our time-space relationship must necessarily alter in exact accordance with the requirements of the microcosmos."

"And the return? Getting back to our own world, I mean."

Minott was already busy with the connection; between the two mechanisms. He did not look up from his work as he replied, "Oh, for the initial visit I shall set a time switch to control our apparatus here. We'll stay but two minutes and then return in the same manner. After the first trip, a better method can be worked out. But in any event it is merely a reversal of the original process. Are you ready?"

He looked at the younger man with a twinkle in his eye.

"Now? Right away, you mean?"

"Yes. All is prepared."

"Why sure, I'm ready if you are."

"Very well, then. We'll be off at once."

He made the final adjustments to the apparatus, directing the reflectors of the Rollin mechanism to include a tiny disc he had attached to the super-microscope. Grayson was somewhat apprehensive as he watched the attaching and setting of the time switch, but he had no thought of reconsidering or of objecting.

"All right, Gray," Minott said in measured tones, straightening up from the completion of his task.

He drew the younger man into the proper position before the apparatus and threw an arm affectionately over his shoulder as he reached forth with his free hand to close the main switch and press the button. This time it seemed to Grayson that the very fibres of his being were wrenched asunder. There was a terrific flash of blinding light, an inconceivably violent explosion, and then a momentary impression of being hurled through the vastness of space. He opened his eyes to the glare of sunlight and instinctively ducked his head at the sight of a heavy object rushing to meet him. There was a sickening thud and his senses left him completely.

CHAPTER THREE
A Fatal Error

WHEN Grayson R36B recovered consciousness it was slowly and with tortuous, futile attempts at raising himself to a seated position. He lay prone in some feathery, aromatic substance that was soft as down, but of so great a depth as to almost bury his body. His head ached abominably and his lids refused to open at first. Then suddenly he remembered, and he sat up quickly. He drew his hand across his forehead and brought it away covered with blood. Something had gone amiss with their experiment.

A feeble moan at his side caused him to search through the fuzzy substance that carpeted this strange realm and he came across the figure of his friend, Minott V8CA. He had been injured likewise, but they soon discovered that nothing more serious than broken scalps and minor bruises had been sustained by either. Then they arose and had their first sight of the new surroundings.

It was a brown and green landscape that met their view—not greatly unlike the countryside of their own world as it had existed many centuries previously when it was thinly populated. The sward beneath their feet was of great depth and it was fine-stranded and soft like a woman's hair. But it was green—a warm yellow green that was pleasing to the eyes of these city-bred mortals. At the edge of the clearing in which they stood there was a fringe of tall plant life closely akin to the trees of their own world.

These had smooth trunks of a reddish brown hue and rose for a considerable distance before branching into foliage. The foliage itself was of the same warm green as the grass and massed about the tops of the trunks in round, symmetric clusters. The air was balmy and warm—a gentle breeze stirred the soft carpet of the clearing into rippling waves that lapped at the shadows of the forest like the swells of a calm sea.

"What a beautiful place!" exclaimed Grayson. "But how is it that we were thrown here so heavily and that we did not arrive at the point on which the ray was focused? There was a lake at that point, with a sandy beach and with habitations visible in the near distance."

Minott rubbed his bruises ruefully. "I see it all now," he exclaimed. "When we combined the Rollin apparatus with the super-microscope, the ray was deflected an infinitesimal amount by the introduction of our hyper-physical entities. We are probably quite some distance from the point of original focus and at quite a different elevation on the miniature world. That is why our landing was not so gentle."

Grayson had glanced at the sky and he gasped in utter amazement: "Why, there are three suns in the heavens!" he cried.

AND such was the case. One shone hotly red and was exactly overhead. The other two, of smaller size, shone paler and with a colder light. These two were close together but fully fifteen degrees from the first and the net result in lighting their surroundings was a brilliance seemingly even greater than that of their own sun and of similar quality as regards color of the light. The multiple shadows lent a strange triple complement to their movements.

"Yes, I expected that," replied Minott. "This atom, which is now our universe, contains quite a number of protons of which these three are self luminous. If it were an atom of gold, whose atomic number is 79 and the atomic weight 197, there would be 79 protons in the nucleus. In addition there would be 118 protons to make up its weight as well as 118 electrons to neutralize these 118 protons. About the nucleus there would be 79 additional electrons to neutralize the 79 protons comprising the atomic number. Of course this universe is a much less complex one than an atom of gold, but it is far more complex than an atom of hydrogen, which consists of but one proton with a single electron to neutralize it."

"Then we must expect many things to be different than those existing at home?"

"Yes indeed, and interestingly so. And do you know, Grayson, we must make up our minds to remain in this place for we shall never be able to return to earth."

"What! We can't return?"

"No. I was far too optimistic in my setting of the time switch. According to my watch we have been here nearly thirty minutes already, we were probably unconscious for a third of that. The apparatus has long since functioned and we are still here. Of course the ray of the super-microscope having been deflected from its true course by our advent, we were lost to it on its return, for it would impinge at the point of original focus, which point we missed. We are doomed to remain."

Grayson gazed gloomily at his mentor. "Fine fix we are in," he commented.

"Yes. And it's all my fault for being too precipitate and not taking time to prepare more carefully."

The great scientist was so crestfallen that the young man burst into laughter. He threw an arm about the older man.

"After all," he said. "What does it matter. We have but little at home that we may not have here. Since both mother and father are gone I have no one but you—and I still have you. There is your home and position, of course, but insofar as family ties are concerned you are similarly situated. And we can make a place for ourselves right here. Probably we shall be better off."

"Bravely spoken my boy," said Minott, with an answering hug. "And now suppose we explore a bit and orientate ourselves."

Undismayed, they set forth toward the forest.

For two hours they tramped through the unfamiliar multi-shadowed depths of the wood, stopping often to examine some new growth that was discovered. It appeared to be a trackless jungle, peopled only by furred and feathered creatures of small size and timid nature. Then suddenly they came out upon a road, a smooth highway of glistening metal that wound its way through the forest.

"Well, this is encouraging," said Minott. "All roads lead somewhere—in both directions. Which shall we try?"

"The forest looks thinner to the right. Why not that way?"

"All right. Let's go."

With little thought to the future they trod the silvery road for several miles, as they would judge distance on earth. They were nearing the edge of the wood and were suddenly in the open.

The three suns had sunk so low that the two smaller ones were close to the horizon. The period of the first twilight was about to set in, but ahead of them in the slanting rays, there gleamed a magnificent city, a city of towering walls and great spires and domes, all constructed of the silvery metal on which they walked.

They stood spellbound for a moment before advancing further. Each was so impressed with the grandeur of the sight that neither spoke a word. Then there came a ringing command. Each was sure that no sound had broken the stillness, yet that command was heard as surely and clearly as if shouted in their ears.

"What was that?" asked Grayson in astonishment.

"You heard it too? It was a distinct command to stop, though I am sure there was no speaker."

"Exactly as it seemed to me."

Undecided they remained rooted to the spot for a space. Then Grayson took an experimental step. Again came that insistent demand and he withdrew the foot he had thrust forward.

Then there came a roar from the skies and a huge cylindrical vessel swooped directly before them, alighting on the metal surface of the road as lightly as a bird. The voice that was not a voice spoke to them once more.

"Approach closely," it commanded.

They obeyed in some little trepidation, drawing near to the strange conveyance and stopping as a small square opening appeared in the side nearest them.

"Enter," cam

They stepped through the opening into the cylinder.

CHAPTER FOUR
In a New World

THE darkness sprang into intense light as the door closed behind them. Blinded to the point of hypnosis, they saw nothing but eyes—eyes that glared and stared; inspected them as if they were laboratory specimens of an infinitely inferior sort.

Then that blinding light was gone—gone so suddenly that the darkness seemed terrifying. But it was not for long. The unspoken voice came once more. "They are different!" it said.

Soft hands laid hold on them, flabby fingers pawed their bodies.

"Ugh!" protested Grayson.

Then they were in a room of comfortable brightness and warmth. Six pairs of the eyes regarded them, and for the first time they were aware of the features in which those all-seeing, all-knowing optics were set. These were not the creatures they had viewed through the super-microscope. Far from human was their appearance. But there was more of intelligence—of sinister cunning and evil intent in those blue-rimmed eyes than in the most despicable and villainous of mortals. The heads were hairless and somewhat globular, the gray skin drawn in folds over their ugly skulls. Ears they had none—nor mouths—nor chins. Nothing there was that marked them as human; save those eyes—and these were superhuman in their penetrating quality and discernment.

Again there came the voice that sounded not: "Creatures of exceptional knowledge," it said, "whence came ye? Surely not from the savage tribes of Els, nor from Pra or its satellites. In our solar system there are no other inhabited planets. Then, whence came ye?"

Grayson and Minott stared at one another without making reply. Each had understood the questions propounded, yet neither comprehended fully, nor had they heard an uttered sound.

"Reply!" came the command. "Full well we know that thy lesser intelligences are incapable of communicating with such as we, on the terms of equality. Yet, from the impulses that come to us, we are aware how ye communicate one with the other. Ye are possessed of antiquated organs, ears, lips, bronchial tubes, like the Elsians. Speak then, that we may read thy thoughts."

The older man was struck dumb, but Grayson's youthful vigor asserted itself in rising anger.

"We are from Earth," he said, "on a friendly mission. And we are astonished at the unfriendly reception we have been accorded."

"Earth?" came the voice that was unbearable. "Why speakest thou that which is untrue? Thy words, though we hear them not, convey to our superior minds meanings that are false."

MINOTT nudged his impetuous partner into sullen silence.

"Earth, as we call it," he repeated in a conciliatory voice, "is a planet of another and far away system. My friend speaks the truth. We are from Earth, and we have no enmity against the peoples of your system."

"Thou liest as well! There is but one other system—the system of Oc, and that is so far distant as to be unreachable."

Grayson and Minott felt themselves seized by forces of great power and of unknown source and nature. They struggled to no avail. There was a quick jerk that threw them to the hard floor, and they knew the ship was in motion. The light and the penetrating eyes were gone and they felt about in the darkness until they found each other.

"Well, this is a fine welcome!" exclaimed Grayson.

"Yes, and the worst of it is that these beings aren't even inhabitants of the world we came to visit. What they're doing here I don't know, but they're not the people we saw through the super-microscope and it seems they are as unfriendly to them as they are to us. What the object of the enmity may be is another thing."

There was a sudden swift descent of the vessel, a crash, and it came to rest. Windows opened on two sides of the room they occupied and through the thick glass, or whatever transparent medium it was, they saw that the ship had descended in the city of gleaming metal. They became aware of great activity within and of much clamor without. A cloud of dense vapor obscured their vision for a time, during which period the activity within increased and they could hear heavy footsteps and the moving about of bulky objects. The mist cleared and they saw a mass of red-gowned humans—humans like themselves, with perfectly formed featured. But this mass of beings lay in pitiful heaps in the center of a great square where there was no other living thing save three of the earless, mouthless, large-eyed creatures who poked about among the bodies. They were removing the valuables from the persons of those unfortunate victims of the deadly gas.

The blinding light from within assailed them suddenly and, blinking dazedly in its glare, they saw five of the red-gowned humans thrust into their own cell and thrown to the floor. The artificial light vanished as suddenly as it had come—then the daylight as well, for slides of some sort were drawn across the transparent windows.

"Wonder if we can make ourselves understood to these other prisoners," said Grayson.

There was a reply, another wordless communication, a mental impression transmitted from the mind of one of these beings.

"We understand," it conveyed. "You have but to speak for a few minutes and we shall be able to converse with you in your own tongue. Proceed."

Minott spoke slowly and distinctly. "Grayson," he said, "this is a remarkable demonstration of telepathy. Those of the great eyes possess the same power, but something tells me these Elsians, as I presume our fellow prisoners are called, have the keener intelligence though they are apparently at the mercy of the great-eyes. The ship is moving once more and I suppose we are being conveyed as captives of war along with these five who have just been incarcerated with us."

He spoke for perhaps five minutes along the same lines. Then he was interrupted by a gentle voice, a voice of singing quality that pronounced his own uncouth English in accents that made of it a language of smooth beauty.

"You have spoken truly," came the voice from out the stygian darkness, "and sufficiently to enable us to be able to converse with you. We have, over a period of time, learned the mental communication of the Prags—the great-eyes as you humorously termed them. But such communication is forbidden in all Els. We prefer the spoken word, as we do not wish to evolve as the Prags have—the pirates who prey on the entire universe and who have become hideous in appearance. From where do you come—one of the satellites of Pra?"

"No," Minott responded. "We come from another solar system—from a planet called Earth."

"From the system of Oc?" asked the gentle voice.

"No, from still further."

"Further than Oc?" The voice was frankly astonished now, but not incredulous.

"Yes, much further than Oc. As we measure distance in our land, it is but a fraction of an inch to our own home, but in your terms, which we know not, it is an unthinkable distance."

There was puzzlement in the reply and Grayson nudged his friend into silence. At that moment the blue glare of the lights dazzled them once more, and one of the Prags entered the narrow chamber. Then there was a gradual softening of the brilliancy until the Earth visitors were able to make out clearly the ugly form of the Prag.

The short body, surmounted by the immense bulbous head that seemed to be all eyes, was clothed in a single baggy garment of leather through which the emaciated arms and legs projected. At the waist, the garment was drawn together by a somewhat broad sash, from which descended a wickedly curved knife and a glittering mechanism that appeared to be a hand weapon of some sort. The lidless eyes with their strange blue rims and bloodshot intensity peered through and through the prisoners from the earth.

"You are to appear before the Kama," they were commanded by the thoughts of this creature.

Minott and Grayson, without volition and propelled by a power from without their consciousness, rose meekly and followed the Prag from the room, leaving behind them the softly muttering Elsians.

CHAPTER FIVE
Silent Commands

THE Kama proved to be the commander of the swiftly moving ship and he faced them in a forward compartment whose transparent sides revealed to them the glories of the sub-universe through which they were traveling. From the mind of this officer there came the command to observe the heavens, and he watched them narrowly as they gazed through the windows.

Far below them was a swiftly receding orb that they knew was the planet Els, from which they had been abducted. The super-microscope had shown them a similar view of the sphere. But there all familiarity ceased, for they had not shifted the focus of their instrument after discovering the one inhabited electron. To the left there shone the three suns, the red one displaying a magnificent corona of flaming streamers that dazzled them with its glory. The two smaller suns, those of the cold light, had no coronas but shone with the wavering radiance of enormous mercury vapor lights. The firmament was of ebon blackness and was dotted with no less than fifteen major bodies and countless more distant stars and nebulas. Ahead of them there loomed a rapidly nearing body that shone with a yellow light and about which revolved two smaller bodies, one of a greenish hue and the other the same tint as the parent body. The speed of the pirate vessel must have been terrific, for the shifting of size and position of the visible bodies was inconceivably rapid. They would arrive at their destination very soon indeed.

"It is as I thought," the mental message of the Kama interrupted their thoughts. "My Prags were mistaken. Thou hast told them truth. Thy thoughts are entirely unfamiliar with this system as well as with Oc, the island universe out beyond the twenty-seven planets. For this thou shalt be saved and shall commune with the scientists of Pra. Long have they theorized on the possible existence of universes within universes, of matter divided and sub-divided to the point where little exists save empty space. Thou comest from a vaster universe wherein our system is but an infinitely small particle. Is it not so?"

Minott stared agape. "It is true, Kama," he said, "but little did we think to find theories similar to our own in this realm, nor to find a combination of savagery and enlightenment such as the inhabitants of Pra seen to have. What is the meaning of it all?"

"It is an inheritance from the distant past," came the unspoken reply. "Not all inhabitants of Pra are Prags, as we are termed by the Elsians, but the Prags are the rightful rulers of our universe. It has been thus from time immemorial. But ruling the universe in peace is an impossible accomplishment. Therefore we, the chosen few, dominate by force the remote provinces of Pra itself and the entire universe of which it is part. This we do by swooping down on the provinces regularly, levying tribute in the form of manpower and of wealth. It is divine inheritance, a privilege none can gainsay. By the outlanders we are cursed and feared, are termed buccaneers, pirates, freebooters. Yet it is our right. The Prags must exist not by labor but by their superior mentality. The inferior races of our system must pay constant homage and provide us with the living and luxuries that are ours by divine right."

"You meet with no resistance?" asked Minott.

"Occasionally. But it is futile. The outlanders are not sufficiently clever to outwit the omnipotent, omniscient Prags."

Grayson sputtered his wrath. "Of all the conceited, vicious tommy-rot I ever listened to, this is the vilest. The Prags are nothing but drones—drones that sting however, and that live by the labors and sufferings of the less fortunate. Possibly those ugly skulls of yours contain more gray matter, but the Elsians have the better qualities. They have kindness, love, and tolerance in their make-up, whereas the Prag is utterly devoid of the finer feelings. It is a disgusting exhibition of evolution as a coldly scientific proposition—without pity, without tenderness, without love. Instead of the gods you have set yourselves up to be, you are monsters that should be destroyed. Would that some power could blast you from the universe; destroy your ugly bodies and minds—not your souls, for you have none."

Grayson breathed hard as he concluded. Minott feared mightily for the result of this bitter speech. But the unspoken reply was without rancor.

"Thou hads't done better to save thy breath," it came through to their minds. "Your feelings are known. The mental attitude registers with us far more easily than useless speech, which we cannot hear. But it is pardoned; it is expected; it is merely the hatred of the slave for its master. However, you two will prove interesting and valuable to our Great Ones, whom you shall soon visit. From them you can hide nothing."

There was no adequate reply, so the two earthmen remained mute, staring moodily at the great shining sphere that now loomed so large in the heavens. The Kama nodded and the Prag who had brought them to his presence came in and led them back to their cell.

A voice greeted them from the darkness as the do or clanged to behind them, the soft voice that now spoke their language.

"What is to be your fate?" it inquired solicitously.

"We are to meet the Great Ones, whosoever they may be," replied Grayson. "We are to tell them of the world from which we come and to discuss science with them."

"That is a far happier fate than ours," came the gentle voice. "You should be thankful that your lives are not to be sacrificed in the mines and workshops of the Prags, as are ours. We have no hope."

"Is that what becomes of the captives from your land?" asked Minott. "Surely the few of you who are with us in this cell wouldn't be sufficient excuse for the raiding trip of this immense ship."

"We are doomed to hard labor under conditions of such grueling severity that our lives are shortened to less than half their normal span," spoke the voice. "And as to the number of the captives, we five are but a small proportion. There are four great prison cells in these vessels. Each contains one hundred Elsians. We five are merely an overflow and were thrown in this small cell with you two because there was not enough room. They have also brought large quantities of precious metals from our city."

"What rotten scoundrels they are!" exclaimed Grayson. "Do such raids occur often?"

"Only often enough to replenish their stores and to replace the workers who have died off in their misery. But there is also the raid, or rather the expected visit, when they compel us to give up three hundred of our fairest maidens. This occurs once during each revolution of Els."

"Once a year," exclaimed Grayson. "Good grief, do they take your women for mating purposes?"

"No. Merely for their amusement—to grace their debauches and orgies, and to die, before their time, of shame and of physical decay brought about by the life they are forced to lead. No, the Prags do not mate with our women. That would pollute the strain they have so carefully evolved through eons of time."

"Horrible!" exploded Grayson. "Can't anything be done to forestall them? Have you not retaliated? Can you not organize manpower and materials to destroy these beasts?"

"Hush!" replied the Elsian. "We must not speak of such things. Our every word may even now be going on record and be used against us. There are plans, but we must not speak of them."

Grayson and Minott shivered with horror at the tale of the Elsian. Neither replied. And then they felt a retardation of the speed of the vessel. It came to a sudden stop.

"We are about to land," spoke the invisible Elsian.

"Yes, in the land of the Prags," said Grayson, with loathing in his voice.

CHAPTER SIX
The City of the Prags

THE scene on the landing stage in the city of the Prags will remain forever impressed on the minds of the two Earthmen. A vast, mirror-like surface it presented and there were gathered thousands of the misshapen creatures to welcome the return of the raiding vessel with its load of treasure and prisoners. The sea of pink, upturned expanses of flesh that were containers merely for the huge brains and the staring optics overcame them with nausea. To think that these monstrosities were in the ascendancy over the handsome and kindly Elsians!

They were sickened at the brutal handling of their more than four hundred fellow prisoners and Grayson cried his rage aloud at sight of a number of aggravated cases in the prodding and beating of stragglers and rebellious captives. The three suns shone on the scene with even greater brilliance than they had in Els—evidently Pra was considerably closer. The atmosphere was heavy and foul as opposed to the sweet-scented, invigorating air of Els. There was a haze over everything and the humidity was such as to bring beads of perspiration to the brows of the Earthmen. In perfect uniformity on all sides of the great landing stage, there rose towering buildings of ebon blackness—not the glossy black of jet, but a dead, lifeless charcoal that reflected so little light as to cast a pall of gloom about them.

In the confusion created upon the landing and the disposal of the Elsian prisoners, Grayson and Minott had drawn aside unhindered and apparently unnoticed. They were now approached by the Kama and, by exercise of his will, he compelled them to follow him. They walked through staring crowds of the detestable Prags and entered one of the gloomy buildings at the edge of the landing stage.

No hand was laid on them, yet they were forced to proceed in the desired direction as inexorably as if they had been bound and carried. They were taken into a lift, which soon bore them to the uppermost portion of the structure. There, on the top level under a vast expanse of the transparent material used in the windows of the ship, they were brought to the Great Ones. The huge compartment was a veritable conservatory. It bloomed with strange and rank vegetation. Tall, serpentine growths of ghastly gray hue spread sickly fronds to the uppermost heights under the transparent covering overhead. The earthmen wrinkled their nostrils in revulsion at the offensive odors of the plant life that was evidently admired by the Prags. They moved slowly through a passageway between the growths and soon reached a sort of dais on which there were three cushioned divans set in triangular formation in the full glare of the Pragian sun. On these reposed the Great Ones.

Mere brains were the Great Ones. Their bodies were shrunken beyond all belief and the huge, semi-transparent heads lay helpless amongst the cushions, the immense eyes presenting the only evidence of life in the weird beings.

The Kama bowed low and young Grayson and Minott perforce followed suit, though they raged inwardly. In stupefied silence they peered into the eyes of the Great

Ones, and, for the first time, Grayson observed the nature of the blue rims about the unblinking orbs of these, the highest type of Prags. They were porous areas, and the minute pores opened and closed rhythmically! They were the breathing organs of the uncouth things! But the discovery detracted not one whit from the hypnotic effect of the bloodshot eyes.

"Beings from the great outside universe," came the thoughts of one of the Great Ones, they knew not which, "you come at an opportune time. We have but recently discovered the existence of your universe and would learn more of its extent and peculiarities from recent dwellers therein. We would likewise know how your advent into our system was accomplished. Speak…"

Minott replied, "Our universe is to yours as is yours to a grain of sand by the seashore. We entered by means of an extremely powerful microscope and the fourth dimension."

"Thy first statement is understood and conceded. But as to the second, there is some doubt. Concentrate on this instrument of which thou speakest, that we may read of its construction and operation."

Grayson exploded, "Don't do it, Minott. The beasts will try to reverse the process and enter our own system."

"Objections are useless," replied Minott to his hot-headed ward. Then he continued in an elaborate description of the super-microscope while Grayson fumed and fretted at the seemingly indiscreet speech of the scientist.

"It is well," came the approving thoughts of the Great Ones. "Thou hast the intelligence to know that the information should have been purloined from thy very brain hadst thou not given it willingly. But it is enough for the present. We shall commune further at a later time.

Meanwhile thy friend is condemned to the mines. He is of inferior intellect."

Minott protested sorrowingly. Grayson endeavored to attack the monstrosities that lay so smugly among their cushions, but the mysterious power once more gripped him and he was led helpless from the presence of the Great Ones, Minott's eyes followed sadly.

THE treatment accorded the scientist was greatly different. At a command from the Great Ones, two slaves entered their presence and were ordered to convey him to certain living quarters. To Minott's delight, these slaves were Elsians who had kindly human countenances, and seemed overjoyed at being permitted to serve a creature so like their own kind.

He was conveyed to rooms that, but for the difference in colors and kinds of materials used, might have been in his own land. But he walked the floor with his mind constantly on Grayson. The two Elsians stood aside patiently, as they observed the dejection of their new master.

Clearly to him then came the mental message, "You are worried about a friend?"

Minott peered startled at the nearest of the Elsians who was smiling commiseratingly. Why, uh—yes," he said hesitatingly. "My friend from another world, who has been condemned to the mines."

"Speak further," came the encouraging message. And Minott poured out his heart to the gravely listening Elsians. He told of Grayson's childhood, of his later life, of the experiment that had brought them to Els and resulted in their capture by the Prags. He concluded with a hopeless note, as he told of the scene in the place of the Great Ones.

"Fear not," the voice came in perfect English when he had finished, "the time is close at hand. Grayson will be rescued, as will all of our people when the great day comes. You have but to be patient and obey all of the commands of the Great Ones. Through our secret system of communication, we shall learn of the whereabouts of your friend and arrange for the interchange of messages between you and him."

Minott was astounded at the facility with which this Elsian had learned his own tongue—more easily than had the first in the spaceship. But he was elated at the hope held forth and was about to make eager reply when there came an insistent buzz from close by.

One of the Elsians left the room hurriedly and the other—the one who had spoken—laid a warning finger to his lips and busied himself with the appurtenances of a dressing table. Minott knew not what to expect.

There was complete silence for a moment. Then two Prags entered the room, bearing between them a golden sphere of the diameter of a large pumpkin. With a curt nod from one of them, the Elsian servant was dismissed and they set the shimmering globe on a table.

Drawn to the beautiful polished object by an irresistible force, the scientist found himself gazing into depths of wavering brightness that soon resolved into scenes on the other electron planet, Els. With great rapidity the scenes shifted, outlining in rapid succession an entire continent and picturing city after city similar to the one they had first seen. Rural districts were also covered, particular attention being paid to the vicinities of small bodies of water. Then suddenly he recognized the locality they had been observing through the super-microscope. His start of recollection brought about the immediate cessation of the action of the sphere and a mental message came at once from one of the Prags:

"It is well. The location of the ray is determined."

They marched solemnly from the room without further ado, taking the golden sphere with them. The clang of the door as they left brought a sense of dire foreboding to Minott and he stared helplessly about the lonely rooms.

CHAPTER SEVEN
Among the Elsians

FOR several days Grayson labored with pick and shovel in an underground passage that was so narrow and stifling that he was too exhausted each night to even think of the fate that had befallen him. The material he was wresting from narrow veins in the damp wall of rock was radioactive—no light was needed in these workings—and he knew that his life would be short indeed if he were forced to continue in this place. He had been put into the most dangerous of all the mines. But the physical presence of the Prags was escaped during the long hours of labor, and this was a relief of a sort, though the force of distant wills kept him doggedly at his task. The Prags never entered the diggings where the mineral that supplied them with their main source of energy was obtained.

Then came a day when the Elsian who worked next to him spoke to him in his own tongue. A message had come from above—a message from Minott! It was wonderful!

The scientist was well, it seemed, and wished to inform his friend that powerful forces were at work that would eventually bring about their release from Pra and their return to Els. He was bidden to keep courage.

"But," asked Grayson, "how has this message been relayed to you?"

"By word of mouth entirely. It has passed on from an Elsian servant of your friend and has undoubtedly been repeated a score of times on its way to this remote working. We have perfected among the captives a secret system of communication that serves the purpose admirably, though it is somewhat slow."

"The message gives word of help to come," said Grayson. "What does this mean ?"

"It means this," replied Oril, for that was the cognomen of his new friend. "The prisoners on this accursed island have formed plans that will eventually result in the destruction of the Prags and in the liberation of themselves. They will result in the halting of the age-long piracy to which our worlds have been subjected, and in the salvation of the civilizations that have for so long a time been under the lash."

"By what means is this to be done?"

"I cannot divulge the secret until you have been admitted to our council. But this will be soon, and I can tell you that the vulnerability of the Prags has been discovered, and that Els and the two satellites of Pra, as well as the outlying provinces of Pra itself, are banded together to end the dominance of these creatures once and for all."

"You spoke of an island," said Grayson. "Do you mean that the Prags inhabit no part of this planet except a single island?"

"That is correct. The island is known to us as Capis and it comprises less than one tenth of the total habitable surface of Pra. The outlying provinces are populated sparsely and by a miserable race of downtrodden creatures, who were subject to the banditry of the Prags for ages, before they discovered the means of traversing space and transferred their major activities to the other inhabited bodies of our system. The provinces have been bled dry and the peoples are hopelessly retarded in their civilization.

They resemble us in appearance, though their skin is of much darker hue, and in some sections they have almost reverted to savagery. But all of that is to be changed also."

"This council of which you spoke. When and where does it meet?"

"At present there is a meeting every night in one of the deepest levels of the mines. But each night those present are a different group and word of the proceedings is carried over to the next night by a single member who thus attends two meetings in succession,. This is necessary in order that the Prags shall not suspect us of such activities as they surely would, if any considerable number of us were absent from our quarters on a single evening. Of course we are aided in this by the fact that they feel absolutely secure in their diabolic tyranny over us, and so do not anticipate a rebellion of serious nature. They underestimate the courage and mentality of the long-suffering outlanders, and are thus thrown more or less off guard by their own colossal conceit."

The conversation was interrupted by the shrill siren that called the workers to the evening meal—the siren that told them of the completion of the long day of labor. The two were soon in the great bucket that carried them to the surface, along with some fifty more of their fellow prisoners.

GRAYSON pondered over the things he had heard all through the nightly inspection and during the meal that was presided over so strictly by a number of lower class Prags. These were not of the type that possessed the intense power of will over the prisoners, but enforced their will by free use of the lash and in aggravated cases of insubordination, by the use of the ray pistols they carried at their belts. Grayson had once seen one of these weapons used and he carried horrified remembrance of its action in his mind. The unfortunate victim of the crackling blue flare that greeted a minor insolence, had crumpled before his eyes into a heap of putrefaction that rapidly shrank to complete and terrible dissolution. He shuddered anew at the thought and was unable to finish his food.

But the words of Oril had cheered him, though he was doubtful of the ability of the Elsians and other outlanders to conquer these monstrosities, who were possessed of such marvelous mental powers and had evidently been lords of the tiny universe for ages of time.

Later in the evening, when the three suns had set and the prisoners were herded to their underground quarters. Grayson received word from Oril that he was expected to attend the meeting of the council to be held late that night. He was elated over the news and could scarcely remain quietly in his bunk until the time set for his adventuring forth from the huge bunk room into the dark passages where he was to be led to the meeting place of the conspirators. Oril had given him explicit directions and he knew that he would have no trouble in joining the guide who was to await him. His neighbors were asleep on the low cots that were provided by the Prags in all the bunkrooms, and the lone guard was nodding in the dim-lit corner of the long hall. The faint whimpers of a sick prisoner, a few cots from his own, had ceased and Grayson hoped that the poor devil had found relief from his sufferings in the mercy of death.

Then there was the padding of soft footsteps and in the dim light he saw that two of the upper class Prags had entered and were conferring with the guard, who had started guiltily from his nap at their approach. The newcomers were led through the long aisle and Grayson's heart missed a beat as they neared him where he lay. He feigned sleep and when the brilliant beams of a hand torch were turned upon him he opened blinking eyes to their glare. He was discovered as a conspirator, and would never know the plans of the brave band, which was setting out to free the worlds they knew from the iron hand of the oppressor!

There was the single command to follow, so he arose from his hard couch and obeyed the order in silence. There was nothing else he could do.

He was conducted to the surface and taken to a small, brightly-lighted landing stage where one of the tiny, bird-like air vehicles of Capis awaited. In a moment they had winged their way aloft and were headed for the lights of the city of the Great Ones. What was to be his fate Grayson did not know, nor did he much care—now. He had scented adventure and it was to be denied him. He had hoped to engage in the battle for freedom that Oril had hinted was coming. But he was quite evidently doomed to disappointment and worse.

The drone of the motor and the swish of the flapping wings of the vessel that carried them swiftly toward the city were the only sounds to disturb his train of gloomy thought. The Prags, mute always, did not explain by mental message the reason for his move from the mines back to the city. But he suspected that his and Oril's conversation were known to the Great Ones and that he was to answer to them for his part in it.

Beneath them circled the lights of the great city as the ship swung around to effect a landing. The motor had stopped and they swooped with a rush toward a black square that was outlined by a fringe of orange light. It rushed upward to meet them and it seemed they would surely crash. Then there was a single powerful beat of the broad wings and the little craft alighted without a jar. Below them was the transparent roof of the headquarters of the Great Ones.

CHAPTER EIGHT
Grayson Comes Back

GRAYSON, with rebellion and fury in his heart, neared the throne where lay the three arch-pirates of the atom universe; He longed to lay hands on one of the vile creatures and tear him limb from limb. And when he saw the haggard face of his friend Minott, who sat at a small table adjacent to the dais, he clenched his fists, as if about to carry out his rash desire. Quick as a flash there came the paralyzing of the muscles that was produced so easily by some mental process of the ghastly creatures, and a single unspoken warning that seemed to come from within his own consciousness:

"Cease thy futile ragings," came the adjuration. "The plans of the Great Ones have altered to thy good. No longer shalt thou labor in the mines. This night you shall depart for Els in one of our space ships and in the company of thy friend. Minott has been of much assistance to us and in gratitude we have granted his wish that thou mayst be permitted to join him in this expedition of our scientists. That is all."

Grayson's tense muscles relaxed. Then they did not know of his talk with Oril! But he cast the thought from his mind at once, fearing to betray himself to their uncanny faculties. Minott smiled wanly and greeted him with open arms. Evidently he too had suffered and continued to suffer.

They were dismissed immediately by the Great Ones and retired to Minott's quarters to prepare for the journey.

"What's it all about?" asked Grayson, when their affectionate greetings were over.

"It is a plan to attack our own world," came the hopeless reply, "and we are to assist them and act as their guides when they reach there—if they do. I was compelled to give them all of my data regarding the super-microscope and the four-dimensional means used by us in reaching this system. They learned from me the location of the ray of my super-microscope where it still impinges on the planet Els at the edge of the lake. Their scientists have calculated that the process can be reversed, and they have constructed a duplicate of the Rollin apparatus in accordance with my description of the mechanism. They reason that they can utilize the ray that still connects the point we were watching in Els with my laboratory at home, and they plan to send one of their spaceships, manned and armed, to our world along this beam."

"Is such a thing possible?" gasped Grayson.

"I fear that it is, my boy. You see the time-space relationship can as well be altered in one direction as in the other. By the same means that we adapted ourselves to conditions on this plane, they should be able to adapt themselves to conditions on our own. I can pick no flaw in their calculations, and I am mortally afraid that this unspeakable banditry of theirs is to be extended to our own country. The worst of it is, we are helpless to prevent them."

"But—but," objected the younger man, "if one of these spaceships of the Prags is rotated into the hyperphysical plane and then emerges in your laboratory, it will be of enormous size. It can not occupy the available space, if it is of the same proportions there as it is here."

"It will burst the walls of the laboratory like a chicken breaking forth from an egg and will lie exposed to the sky amid the debris of a great section that will have been torn from the upper surface of our own New York. You forget that my laboratory is in the extreme upper level and that the walls and floors of our city structure will crumple like glass against the sides of a vessel of more than 1000 feet in length and with walls as hard as steel and of more than five feet thickness—suddenly thrust in their midst as it will be."

Grayson groaned. He was heartsick over the change that had come to the beloved features of his foster father. Minott had aged ten years, it seemed, during the few days they had been in this awful realm. He thought too of the terrible engine of destruction to be let loose on an unsuspecting world—and of others to follow, for the Prags would not stop at one if the initial venture proved to be a success.

"Is there no way of stopping the brutes?" he asked.

"None that I can think of. Of course we must do everything we can to upset their plans, but I am afraid we are helpless."

There came the sound of the buzzer and Minott paled to a still more ghastly color. "It is the signal," he said. "They are ready."

The two earthmen hurried to the great landing stage in the heart of the city and there entered one of the shiny cylindrical vessels, of which Minott had learned there were seven in existence. This time they were not carried as prisoners but as more or less unwelcome, but tolerated guests. They were quartered on the same deck with the nine scientists sent by the Great Ones to complete the plans for sending an expedition into the "Outside Universe." Before they had even settled themselves in their cabins, the ship had taken off and they were on their way to Els. When the Great Ones determined that a thing was to be done, there was little delay in its implementation.

All through the remainder of the night the two men talked, when they should have been resting in their beds. They had been separated for more than a week and each of them had much to tell the other. It was a matter of great speculation between them as to what the plans of the "outlanders" were for the overthrowing of the power of the Great Ones and the destruction of the entire breed of Prags. The slight information given to Grayson by Oril was supplemented by but little more that Minott had learned from his Elsian servants. But it was certain that the outlanders were confident of ultimately ridding themselves of their ancient enemy and that the day for the culmination of their plans was close at hand. Whether it was to come quickly enough to forestall the Prags in this new venture they did not know. And they discussed matters until the Prag vessel slipped into the dawn-brightened atmosphere of Els.

The vessel was soon close to the surface and the Earthmen joined the Prags, who had assembled in the forward compartment, where the transparent floors gave them a full view of the scene beneath and where the rising of the first sun could be seen through the transparent side walls. The first dawn of Els reminded them of moonrise on their own world, for the quality of light was similar, though of greater intensity. It would be several minutes before the second of the cold suns rose and one twelfth of an Elsian day before the red glare of the third sun greeted them. The ship was skimming the surface rapidly at an altitude comparable to about one thousand feet above the surface as measured on Earth, and the peaceful countryside below showed signs of the early activities of the day. Here and there a farmer with his flock of quadrupeds strangely resembling sheep was thrown into a panic at the passage of the pirate vessel, and at several points early travelers in high speed vehicles that traversed the shining roads deserted their cars and fled into adjacent forests in fright at the same vision. But the ship from Pra kept steadily on, and within a short time they saw far ahead a scene that seemed vaguely familiar. Closer they drew and, as the vessel slowed down, they saw they were nearing the lake they had seen through the super-microscope in Minott's laboratory. They were overhead of it in a trice and the great ship circled about to make a landing. Several Elsians who walked by the shore of the lake ran in fright for their homes—mere huts and cabins that were set back a little distance from the shore.

"The point of focus of the super-microscope!" exclaimed Minott.

He looked at Grayson with blanched features and their hearts sank at the realization that they were about to land in this spot, where they would be compelled to assist their captors in preparing for a piratical raid on their own world.

CHAPTER NINE
Preparations in Els

WITH the coming of the pirate vessel to the shore of their lake, the neighboring villagers expected the worst. Knowing there was no escaping the gases and the paralyzing forces of the enemy, they did not attempt to flee the vicinity, but they retreated within doors to postpone their certain doom for as long a time as possible. And when, on the second day, they observed that they were not to be molested, but that the Prags were erecting strange mechanisms in the open outside the spaceship and covering these over with rude shelters, a few of the bolder ones ventured forth from the homes to learn what it was all about. They were still unmolested and they gazed in open-mouthed wonder at the sight of a considerable number of Prags actually at work, laboring with their hands in feverish haste. They were still more astonished to see that the Earthmen, of whom they had heard through the medium of their local news broadcast, were aiding the hated Prags. It seemed that there was some difficulty with the apparatus being erected and they saw that the higher class Prags were greatly perturbed over some unforeseen trouble.

As the days passed and nothing happened beyond occasional relocating of the odd contrivances and further adjustments of their parts, some of the natives went so far as to gather around the scene of activity and watch the proceedings with bold curiosity. Upon seeing that the

Elsians were given little attention by the busy Prags, Grayson made it a point to wander away from the work several times and mingle with the watchers. In this manner he struck up an acquaintance with one Atar, who seemed to be an Elsian of some standing in the community and who mastered Grayson's speech in a very short time as had been done by others of his countrymen. He made friends quickly with the villagers and advised them as to the meaning of the strange proceedings in the open space at the shore of the lake. In turn he was told much of the plans of the outlanders for conquering the Prags and he learned that the day of reckoning was not far off, though it was more than thirty days in the future, and he felt certain that the experiment with the Rollin apparatus and the focus ray of the super-microscope would be successful long before that time.

He told Minott of these things in the privacy of their cabin aboard the space ship and the scientist was deeply concerned over this fraternizing with the Elsians.

"Grayson," he warned, "these Prags are possessed of uncanny faculties and, though they are now so deeply engrossed in the work at hand as to pay little attention, one of the lower class is apt to surprise you in treacherous conversation one of these fine days and you will pay the penalty at the receiving end of one of their horrible dissolution rays."

"I'll be careful. And besides, I like these people and wish to be friends with them. Our case looks hopeless anyway and if I can do nothing to prevent the atrocities of these monsters, I can at least show that my heart is in the right place, until such time as the fate overtakes me that is bound to come sooner or later in any event. How is the work progressing?"

"Well, as you know, the reflectors were reset today and the apparatus readjusted. The energy was tried on a test specimen, one of the small rodents they brought with them, and the result left them more worried than ever. The rodent passed into the hyperphysical plane all right, but was returned fearfully distorted and in a dying condition. This has given them pause."

"You old fox," chuckled Grayson. "I'll bet you threw a monkey wrench in the gears somewhere."

"No," was the solemn reply. "I did nothing of the sort. I must admit, however, that I see a fault in the apparatus about which I have not advised them. Fortunate it is that the Great Ones are not here, for they would have read it out of my mind. These Prags have not the mind-reading faculty to so great a degree as the Great Ones, and I find that I can hide my thoughts from them fairly well."

"Then you think the ultimate success of the project may be delayed for a considerable time?"

"Possibly. But not for long, my boy. These archfiends are devilishly clever and they will stumble onto the difficulty in short order—at least within the next ten days, I should say."

"Is it absolutely certain that the ray of the super-microscope is still in operation?"

"Absolutely. By means of the balvanometers, we have located the exact center of impingement and have mapped the entire circle of its influence, which extends well past the village and outlines the view just as we witnessed it back home. There is no question of the workability of their plan, once the Rollin apparatus is in perfect working condition."

Grayson looked moodily from the open window toward the lights of the village. The sweet breath of the Elsian countryside was wafted to his grateful nostrils. How he wished that conditions were different—that he might be free to roam about as he pleased and explore this inviting planet they had so rashly visited. But the arm of the Prag was long, and he knew he could not get far away if he attempted to escape. Besides there was Minott—and the threatened expedition against his own land.

Through the stillness of the Elsian night there came a faint wavering tremolo—a feminine cry that rose in rapid crescendo to a wailing scream. The two earthmen were electrified to tense expectancy but the cry was not repeated.

"By George!" exclaimed Grayson. "That cry came from the village and I'm going to find out what it's all about!"

"Steady now," admonished Minott. "How do you expect to pass the guard at the door of the vessel?"

Grayson was busy pulling the bedclothes from their bunks. "Not going to," he grunted. "I'm going out the window."

And, all protests of his friend notwithstanding, he made good his statement. Quickly he knotted the sheets and coverlets into a rope of considerable length and this he let out through the open window. Bidding Minott a hasty farewell after tying the makeshift line to the ring used for fastening the window, he let himself down to the ground and made off through the darkness in the direction of the village.

Reaching the fenced-in grass plot that was the gathering place of the small town, he found that considerable excitement centered about the loud speakers of the local news broadcast receiver. A crowd had collected and angry shouts and protests came from every side. A little group in the center of the square was huddled about a prone figure and Grayson pushed his way through until he saw that an extremely beautiful Elsian maiden lay stretched on the grass in a faint. Over her bent Atar, his friend of the past few days.

"What is it, Atar?" he asked, when close enough to get the ear of the obviously agitated Elsian.

"Lola—my daughter Lola," groaned the stricken man. "She has been chosen for the next lot of three hundred. In six days she will be torn from her home and taken to Capis—a slave to the beasts we hate. And in so short a time we would have prevented it!"

Grayson observed the smooth pallor of the girl's skin, her perfect features, the glossy sheen of her hair as it spread over her shoulders where she lay. Then her breast rose and, with a deep sigh, she turned her head in his direction and slowly opened the most wondrous pair of violet eyes he had ever seen. Atar clasped her in his arms convulsively and sobbed like a child.

"By God," swore Grayson, "they'll not get her…"

CHAPTER TEN
Lola

LATE that night Grayson returned to his cabin in the same way he had left, Minott was sleeping the sleep of exhaustion, so he had no one in whom he could confide. But he did not awaken his friend, preferring to fret and toss in his own bunk rather than disturb him. Finally he drifted into troubled slumber, into dreams of the beautiful Lola who had looked at him so pleadingly, dreams of the Prags and of frightful battles with them, in which he fought to protect the lovely daughter of Atar. His tortured mind was not resting for a moment, even in sleep. He dreamed of Minott—dear old Minott—and the scientist seemed to be delivering one of his early talks to the younger man. He told of the composition of matter, of molecules and atoms and electrons—of the universe of the atom where the electrons were the bodies that revolved about the central sun or nucleus. It came to him that an atom was so small, that if magnified as much as ten billion times—the second stage power of the super-microscope—the outer electrons would appear to be as much as three feet from the nucleus, yet the nucleus itself was still no larger than a pin point. It was all a muddle, yet in his slumbers he knew that all these things were actually transpiring on a minute world that was nothing more than an electron in an atom of unidentified matter contained in a grain of sand that lay on the slide of Minott's super-microscope in the New York laboratory.

In the morning he awoke unrefreshed and the first thing he did was to advise Minott of the happenings of the night.

"Worse and more of it," groaned the scientist. "I thought the annual tribute of three hundred girls was not due for forty-five days."

"So did I. That's what I was told, and the day of reckoning was purposely set for a few days before that time to prevent this very occurrence."

"Well, my boy, we're between the devil and the deep blue sea. Here we're helping the brutes in their attempt to raid our own world and at the same time you have gone to work and fallen in love with this Elsian damsel who's about to be abducted. Meanwhile the decent folks of this little universe are about to make a break for freedom and the break will be too late to save your new girl."

Minott's eyes twinkled despite the hopelessness of the situation and Grayson could not repress the flush that mantled his features.

"But what can we do?" he countered. "I'll admit that Lola has made a *great* impression on me…and by George they're not going to get her if I can prevent it. But what can we do?"

Minott spoke solemnly now. "Don't do anything rash, Grayson," he advised. "Keep your eyes open and use your best judgment, but don't forget that we have a powerful enemy to deal with. Our first duty is to our own world, but of course we can do very little to prevent the Prags from carrying out their present plans. Probably the best thing is to submit to things as they are and trust that not too great damage will be accomplished on this initial venture into our universe. Then, when they return from the trip, it will be about time for the action planned by the outlanders and further trouble will thus be averted."

"But dammit, Minott, that doesn't save Lola. And she must be saved, I—I want her."

"You poor boy! Is it as bad as that?"

"Yes." Grayson kicked savagely at the towel he had just dropped.

"Well, run along to the village then and see what you can learn. I'll hold the fort here and—who knows?"

Grayson needed not to be told a second time and the older man watched him with misty eyes as he rushed from the compartment in his haste to be gone.

It was very early and the Prags were late rising, so Grayson didn't anticipate any interference with his leaving the vessel. But when he came to the entrance, he found some little difficulty in convincing the guard that he was merely going for a morning stroll. The guard was one of the lower class of Prags and could not understand the Earthman's thoughts unless he was actually speaking. It seemed that the spoken words, though the Prags heard them not, were a medium that facilitated the telepathic process. And when Grayson turned the latch of the door, this low-class Prag laid violent hands on him. Quick as a flash the earthman had him by the throat and was battering the huge head against the metal partition. The Prag fell unconscious and Grayson, stopping only to take the ray pistol from his belt, rushed from the ship and made for the village.

HE had crossed the Rubicon! He knew his life was now forfeit but he was armed. And he was all his way to Lola, come what might.

Atar met him at the cottage door with a smile on his face and Lola's greeting was such as to cause him to flush with pleasure. The girl was radiant and the father hardly less so, for during the night there had come a message from Arun, capital city of the province, calling all of the three hundred maidens to the city with their parents. It was stated in the message that action was to be taken to prevent the turning over of the annual tribute to the Prags, and this statement accounted for the happiness of father and daughter.

Grayson told of his skirmish with the guard of the vessel and offered to accompany them on their visit to Arun, since it was now necessary for him to leave the vicinity in any event, and he felt that he might be of some service in their company. Atar welcomed the offer and Lola's downcast eyes told of her surprise and pleasure. The earthman's heart sang, though full well he knew that the shadow of death hung over them all. And he fondly patted the ray pistol where it lay hidden in his pocket. He did not worry about Minott, for he knew that the Great Ones considered him too valuable to allow him to be harmed as long as there was still information to be obtained from him regarding the outer universe.

The government ronsal, or road vehicle, that was to call for Lola and her father, arrived in a very short time. It was a car of considerable length, mounted on two wheels of a diameter the height of a man, and completely enclosed in transparent material of crystal clearness. From within there came a musical note that told of the high speed of the gyroscope used for balancing the machine. There were four other girls already on board with their families and with the entrance of Lola and the two men all available space was filled. The ronsal started smoothly and was soon rolling over the surface of the metal road with terrific velocity. Grayson learned that it was but a short run to

Arun—less than one ul, the unit of time that was the twentieth of an Elsian day.

The ribbon of gleaming metal, over which they sped, wound through a beautiful country, but Grayson saw very little of it. He was too busy gazing into those violet eyes and watching the lips of the beautiful girl at his side, as they formed the unfamiliar, yet rapidly learned syllables of his own tongue. So it was that, by the time they had reached the walls of Arun, he and Lola were conversing fluently in English, and he had even picked up a number of words and phrases of the Elsian language. Atar observed these things with approval.

Once within the portals of the huge gate that raised at their approach, they were escorted immediately to a great council chamber where sat the provincial governor and his deputies. A great assemblage of Elsians was there and Grayson thought that almost all of the three hundred chosen beauties had preceded them. But he failed to see a single maiden that could compare with Lola, though all of them were undoubtedly charming.

There was a short wait for a few more arrivals, after which a secretary called the roll. The Governor then arose and spoke rapidly and forcefully in the Elsian tongue, becoming much excited and red-faced during the speech. At its conclusion there came a great cheer from the assemblage and Grayson noticed that tears of joy coursed down the cheeks of Atar. Lola translated to him quickly:

"He says that the government has decided not to let us be sacrificed," she said happily. "The day of reckoning with the Prags is set ahead and is to be tomorrow, instead of as planned. We girls are to be kept in Arun under government protection, and our families as well, while the fighting is going on. The prisoners on Pra have been notified, as well as the inhabitants of the two satellites and those of the outlying provinces of Pra itself."

"Hooray!" exclaimed Grayson. And he grasped Atar by the hand and hurried him to the rostrum, where he requested him to translate his offer of enlistment in the forces of Arun.

There was some staccato questioning by the Governor—equally rapid-fire replies from Atar—and Grayson was accepted.

CHAPTER ELEVEN

Grayson Joins Forces

NEXT morning Grayson was outfitted with the uniform and equipment of an Elsian soldier. He was permitted to retain the ray pistol he had taken from the Prag guard and considerable envy was displayed by his fellows over its possession. He requested that he be allowed to bid farewell to Lola and Atar and this too was granted.

Lola gurgled with delight when she saw him and a big thrill came to him as she hugged his arm in her glee and admiration. Atar bid him an affectionate adieu and thanked him profusely for his help and for the courage his presence and support had lent. When Lola accompanied him to the door of their quarters his cup was full, and he bent suddenly down and kissed her upturned lips. Then, in a sudden panic over his temerity, he raced for the square of Arun where the soldiery was assembling. Had he looked back, he would have known that his caress was not unwelcome.

There was a great hullabaloo in the square, and it seemed that all of the population of the city had turned out to witness the departure of the expedition. For the first time Grayson knew what it was all about.

In the center of the square there were two circular pits and into the mouths of these the soldiers were descending. Each of the pits contained a space flyer that had been built secretly during the preceding two years and there were two others of the same type to set forth from another city of Els. The Prags were to be taken by complete surprise.

Grayson joined his unit and was soon within one of the great spheres that were so different from the projectile-shaped vessels of the Prags. The number carried by each vessel was in excess of five hundred; including crew and soldiery. He was extremely interested in the equipment of the vessel and in the activities of his new comrades. So, when the confusion had subsided and the hatches were battened down, he struck up a conversation with his commanding officer, using his few words of Elsian as an entering wedge. He was much pleased to find that the captain, Erne by name, was able to pick up his own language almost at once as had been done by the others with whom he had come in contact.

The ship was under way in a surprisingly short time, shooting forth from the mouth of the pit like a ball from the bore of an old-fashioned cannon. They were on their way to Pra and Grayson was bursting with curiosity as he questioned the indulgent Erne.

"What is the plan of campaign?" he asked.

"There are four ships leaving Els, two more from Aun and three from Rad. These are the satellites of Pra. It is known that all of the fliers of the Prags are in their own cradles excepting two, one of which is at the shore of Lake Ilo in Els and the other in the province of Trasa in Pra. We will leave our own people at home to deal with the one at Lake Ilo and the outlanders will deal with the one at Trasa. But the nine vessels will attack Capis directly and will be assisted by the prisoners there who are apprised of our coming and of the change in plans."

"But, what weapons are to be used against the Prags?"

"Didn't you know?" asked Erne in surprise.

"No. I had heard vague hints of a recent discovery that was expected to prove effective, but I have no knowledge of its nature."

Erne withdrew from Grayson's belt the cylindrical object, which had been given to him with the rest of his equipment.

"You have not been instructed in the use of the trinor?" he inquired.

"I have not had the opportunity as yet."

The cylinder was of blued metal and by earthly standards Grayson would have judged it to be eighteen inches in length and three in diameter. There was a small catch at one end and Erne pressed this to demonstrate the operation of the weapon. There was a shrill sound from within that rose rapidly in pitch until it was a thin scream. Then it vanished entirely but the weapon still vibrated smoothly to the impulses of some mechanism within.

"The trinor," said Erne, "sets up sound waves or vibrations in the atmosphere. As you noticed, the original sound was audible but gradually rose in pitch until it passed beyond the normal response of your auditory organs. But the trinor is still sending forth powerful waves that disturb the air at the rate of twenty-five thousand cycles per second. These are the waves that will destroy the enemy."

"But how?" asked Grayson. "The Prags can hear no sounds of any frequency."

"True. But you must remember that the Prag was originally equipped with ears and auditory nerves the same as you and I. In the course of his evolution through the ages he learned thought transference and the ears were no longer necessary. After many generations of disuse they atrophied and all outer portions disappeared entirely. But there still remained certain of the inner parts and these are still in existence. Two years ago we had three of the enemies in Arun whom we had taken prisoner during one of their raids and our scientists experimented with them until they learned of their susceptibility to the high frequency air waves. You see it happens that certain tiny bones that are all that remain of the Prag's inner ear lie very close to the great vein that supplies the brain with blood. By subjecting the Prag's body to air waves of the high frequency I mentioned, these bones are set in vibration and, due to their contact with the artery against which they lie, a clot is formed which is carried to the brain and causes almost instant death—apoplexy."

"Capital!" exclaimed Grayson. "But are these small hand weapons the only thing to be used against them?"

"No indeed. Among the prisoners in Capis there are sufficient of the trinors hidden to account for the guards below the surface. These are to be used as soon as our space-fliers reach the island. Then each of the vessels will swoop down upon the city, emitting the waves from great generators that are set in the outer hulls. These will cover considerable areas and will account for many more of the Prags. The prisoners will then rush to the city and the vessels will land at the same time, sending forth their fighting men into the streets. The generators aboard our ships will keep up constant emission of the powerful vibrations and the rest will have to be done by hand to hand fighting. Not a Prag must be allowed to escape."

Grayson thrilled to the call of battle. The closer they drew to the planet of the Prags the more bloodthirsty he became.

"What is our protection against the gases and the ray pistols of the Prags?" he inquired.

"Against the gases we have newly perfected masks, which will be supplied before we land. Against the ray pistol there is nothing. But we hope there will be few left to use such weapons by the time our large generators have gotten in their deadly work."

"What are the odds against us—in numbers I mean?"

"About nine to one including the prisoners. On the ships there are forty-five hundred fighters and there are about twice this number of prisoners in Capis. There are one hundred and twenty thousand Prags, so the ratio I mentioned is approximately correct."

"Thank you, Captain," said Grayson.

A lieutenant was distributing the gas masks and this brought their conversation to an end. The captain busied himself with the radiophone instrument through which his orders were to come, and the soldiers gathered at out the windows where they were able to see the island of Capis with its black central city. The ship was crossing the end of the island and several others of the great spheres could be seen converging on the same point—the city.

There was a sudden vibration accompanying a tremendous, high-pitched scream from somewhere in the ship's vitals. Like the scream of the trinor this rose and vanished, but the vibration persisted. The fight was about to begin!

CHAPTER TWELVE
The End of the Great Ones

GRAYSON felt one of the gas masks thrust into his hand but he was too excited to pay much attention. His face was pressed to the window and he saw that several of the flapping-winged craft of the Prags were approaching their own vessel. So close did they come, that he was able to see the ghastly bulbous heads of the two Prags who occupied the nearest. Then he saw one of them go limp and slump forward in his seat. The second followed suit and the wings flapped crazily, out of control. The bird-like mechanism flew drunkenly and then dashed headlong to earth sending up a cloud of dust as it crashed. The others of the curious squadron quickly joined it and he knew that the wave generators of their vessels were a success.

Along the several roads that entered the city could be seen scurrying groups of Elsians and kindred beings from Rad and Aun. These were the prisoners, rushing from the mines and workshops in accordance with the plan.

Then they were over the city and the nine spheres circled and swooped, their wave generators operating at full capacity. From the square there rose one of the cylindrical Prag fliers and it headed directly toward Grayson's vessel. With a quick spurt the great sphere rose and allowed the pointed metal cylinder to whiz harmlessly past beneath them. It passed so closely that they could hear the rush of its slipstream through the walls of the ship. Then it too went drunkenly reeling, shooting skyward and circling and diving, completely out of control. Again the wave generators had proved their worth. The huge cylinder went down in the midst of the tall ebon buildings, tearing away walls and roof structures and carrying hundreds of Prags to their deaths in the falling debris. Another of the Prag fliers met a similar fate in an attempted attack on another of the spheres of the outlanders. There were cheers from Grayson's companions and one and all they itched to be outside and in the confusion that reigned in the streets of the city.

Still the great spheres circled the city, spreading destruction beneath them. Two more of the Prag fliers rose to the attack and one of the spheres went down at the successful rush of the first of the pointed vessels. But the cylinder was carried to its doom along with the victim for the swift rush had carried the pointed end through and through the sphere where it stuck, the sphere impaled like an apple on a spike. The second cylinder was dodged by its intended prey and soon went down to join its fellows. There remained but one of the ships in the square and the watchers could see that its crew was deserting and making for the buildings on the edge of the square. Grayson's sphere hovered a moment over the square, then settled gracefully to a landing. The order came to don gas masks and the hatches were opened.

Out into the open filed the Elsian infantry, trinors in hand and looking fearfully inhuman with their eyes hidden behind the huge goggles of their masks. Dead and dying Prags lay in heaps about the square and they had to climb over piles of them in places in order to make their way to the streets. A cloud of the white gas descended on them and they fought their way blindly in the direction of the tall building for which they had started. Grayson stumbled over a body and fell heavily. When he arose, he found that he was alone but he staggered his way through the murk until he reached a wall. He felt along this and fell through an opening, which proved to be the entrance of a building. Pushing open the door, he rushed into the corridor, and here there was none of the gas, and the lights were burning brightly. He removed his mask and looked around.

NEITHER Prag nor outlander was in sight and he immediately recognized this as the building that housed the Great Ones. He heard a commotion nearby and walked down the corridor to investigate. In a narrow hall that branched from the corridor he found three of the Elsian prisoners struggling with one of the lower class Prags. As he reached them, there came the crackling blue flare of the ray pistol and one of the Elsians suddenly melted into horrid nothingness. With a cry of rage he drew his own ray pistol, forgetting the trinor, and the Prag turned wide eyes in his direction as the blue flame struck him full in the chest. The two remaining Elsian prisoners were saved and they spurned the shrinking mass of putrefaction that had been their enemy as they rushed to thank their rescuer.

With the assistance of these two slaves he located the lift and the three ascended to the uppermost floor. They emerged under the transparent roof and Grayson grimly set forth to surprise the Great Ones in their den, the two Elsians protesting in fear. He paid no heed to their earnest warnings but proceeded steadily along the aisle between the rank growths that had disgusted him so when they had first reached the place. When he had reached a point about fifty feet from the dais where he was still hidden from the cushions of the Great Ones by foliage, there came the mental command to stop. But instead of retreating at this evidence that the fearsome rulers of the Prags were in their accustomed places, he pressed the catch of his trinor and waited until the whine of its mechanism had risen to the vanishing point. The Elsian slaves retreated precipitately, but Grayson advanced slowly and cautiously in the direction of the dais.

Slowly he felt the paralyzing force creeping over him but he pressed doggedly forward, using every ounce of strength in his body to drag his benumbed limbs into movement. Then he fell heavily to the floor and had to pull himself along by grasping the vines and tree trunks along the path with his stiffening fingers. He was in view of the dais now and he saw that two of the Great Ones had fallen victims to the air vibrations, their colossal, hairless heads having dropped to the cushions on which they rested. But the third, though weakening, was still alive and it was this one that was exerting his will power on the hapless Earthman. With a final desperate effort Grayson twisted that rigid member that was his right arm until he was able to reach the ray pistol in his belt. But he could not aim it in the direction of the remaining Great One. He struggled and fought, but that arm would not move. Then he concentrated with closed eyes. He spoke aloud.

"Grayson R36B," he growled through clamped jaws, "you're not going to let this devil of a Prag get the best of you—you're not. You must lift that arm and blast him from existence—you must—you must!"

Then, miraculously, he found he could move his fingers—a bit at a time he edged, his right arm forward, talking and grunting and berating himself aloud. Then the ray pistol was leveled at the monstrosity that glared at him from among the cushions. Came the blue flare and he was released. His own will power had saved him and he sprang to his feet with a cry of victory. The Elsian slaves came running and they capered in glee at the sight that greeted them from the dais. The power of the Great Ones was no more!

When they eventually reached the square, all of the spherical vessels were landed and the fighting had spread to the side streets. There was not a living Prag in sight and Grayson made his way to his own vessel to report to Erne. He found him at the radiophone and greeted him with a broad smile.

"What have you to report, Grayson," the captain asked.

"I have killed the Great Ones," he replied simply. "What? Killed—the—Great—Ones?" was the incredulous reply. "Alone."

"Alone."

"For that deed you will receive the highest honors and decorations that can be conferred by the Governor-general of Els. You will be famous."

But the Earthman cared not. He was tired and he wanted to go back to Els—to Lola.

CHAPTER THIRTEEN
The Administration Building Gone

FOR three days they remained on the planet Pra, exploring every nook and cranny that might hold a skulking Prag. Communications from Trasa told of the victory over the Prag vessel that was quartered there. The golden sphere told them that the vessel at the shore of Lake Ilo had not been molested, as the Elsians desired to learn more concerning the experiments that were being conducted.

'When Erne told him of this, Grayson groaned. "Captain," he said, "I can tell them all they wish to know of those experiments. And my friend Minott can tell them more. Tell them to destroy the Prags at once by means of the air vibrations. I fear for Minott's safety and I fear for my own world."

"But it is impossible for me to give orders to my superiors," Erne objected.

"Then send one of our ships back. Send me with it and I'll lay the case before the authorities, I tell you Captain, there is much at stake—much."

Grayson was pleading now. He knew that it would be necessary for the greater part of the force to remain in Capis for several more days to make sure the job had been well done. But he pleaded for Minott and for his own people. And eventually Erne took it up with the commander of the expedition. After much explaining on Grayson's part, it was finally arranged that one of the spheres was to return him to Arun and that he was to be allowed to tell his story to the Governor there. He expressed his gratitude in no uncertain terms and hastened to board the vessel that was assigned to carry him back.

During the short voyage he worried constantly. It seemed that the spherical flier was desperately slow, though in reality it made the trip in record time—less than three ul being required.

When they approached the city of Arun, Grayson was in the control room, talking with the pilot. Suddenly he gasped in alarm. The great pointed cylinder that was the Prag's vessel lay crushed in the ruins of what had once been the Administration Building! A vicious curl of white told of the Prag gas cloud that was not yet fully cleared from the streets!

"We are too late!" he moaned. "The three hundred maidens were quartered in that building!"

The pilot looked at him commiseratingly. "You had a sweetheart among them?"

"Yes," Grayson replied. He choked and paled and the pilot maneuvered the ship to as quick a landing as possible.

No sooner were they on solid ground than the Earthman donned his gas mask and demanded that he be allowed to leave the vessel. Upon the pilot's explaining of matters to the captain this was allowed and Grayson rushed into the ruins of the building, crawling under the great metal hull of the Prag vessel to get into the debris. He thought he could locate the chambers where Lola and her father had been quartered and he risked his life in worming his way through caved-in corridors and broken-walled rooms until he reached this point. He found the body of Atar and mourned over it, as if the Elsian had been a life-long friend instead of a recent acquaintance.

But, try as he would, he could find not trace of Lola. He found many other bodies, a few of them of the young girls who were thought so safely homed, but there was no evidence of either the death or the saving of the girl he had loved so quickly and deeply. He crawled from the debris and rushed frantically to the ship that had brought him.

The last vestige of the gas was now cleared away and he found a crowd collected about the entrance of the mammoth sphere. Among them was the Governor, and Grayson elbowed his way to his side. The pilot of the vessel was there and he acted as the Earthman's interpreter.

"Were many of the three hundred saved?" he first asked.

Patiently he waited for the translations. This Governor was not as adept at picking up his language, as had been some of the others.

"Yes. More than two hundred were rescued."

The Governor had a list and he looked through it carefully for the name of Lola. It was not there!

The raid had come unexpectedly, it seemed. Out of a clear sky the enemy had appeared and had laid down gas clouds in several sections of the city. A portable wave generator was finally brought into action and the ship was sent down out of control—unfortunately directly atop the Administration Building. There were thousands of casualties throughout Arun. But the High Command had not suspected that such a thing could transpire.

"Damn the High Command!" said Grayson. "They were wrong, and I have lost Lola—probably Minott too."

He remained in the city, sick at heart. For three days the wrecking crews searched the demolished building, bringing many bodies for identification. But Lola was not among them. When the casualty lists were complete and neither she nor Minott were accounted for, Grayson had an inspiration. Maybe Minott had been left behind! Maybe he was still at Lake Ilo! He would go and find out.

ATTEMPTS to communicate with the village were futile, so the Governor provided a ronsal to carry the Earthman to the village. Before he left, there came the general broadcast advising that the remaining three Elsian spheres had left Pra and were on their way home. The celebration over the complete victory was starting as his ronsal left the city limits, but there was no jubilation in Grayson's heart. He was bitter; brokenhearted.

When the ronsal reached the site of the village they found it in complete ruin. The Prags had destroyed it before they left for Arun! But, looking out toward the lake, it was seen that the huts that covered the experimental mechanisms were still standing. Grayson made all haste to reach them and he searched first one and then the others of the rude shelters.

"Grayson..." came a familiar and beloved voice.

Minott stood before him and the younger man fell to his knees and thanked God that the Prags had left him behind. Minott raised him gently to his feet and led him to the largest of the shelters, thrusting him through the door without a word. There in a chair that they had built when they first came sat Lola!

The young man stopped in his tracks and gazed at her with unbelieving eyes. Then they embraced.

Minott gave them plenty of time, then he stepped through the open door and coughed gently. His face beamed and explanations came fast and furiously.

Half crazed at the death of her father, Lola had made her way to the village only to find it completely in ruins. She collapsed, but by good fortune Minott eventually found her and nursed her back to good health. It was a happy reunion and the three embraced in a huddle from sheer joy.

There came a tremendous wrench, a twisting and warping of the universe, and they stood in Minott's laboratory—three where there had been but two before. Lola still clung to her lover but Minott sprang to the super-microscope and shut off the power.

"What on earth?" gasped Grayson.

Minott glanced at the clock and laughed. "My boy," he said, "our two minutes have expired. Our own apparatus brought us back, thanks to the time switch."

"You mean to say that all of that grief took place during two minutes of our time?"

"Absolutely. The time-space relationship you see. Those long days in the atom universe were but fractions of a second here. The Elsians and the Prags and all of them lived out their lifetimes in less than one of our days. I had forgotten that point while we were there. Which reminds me that I must investigate fully the qualities of our focusing ray. It must have the property of altering the time-space relationship optically, for when we observed the Elsians through the super-microscope their terrific pace of living was not apparent."

"But Lola," objected Grayson, "will she live a normal span of years here?" He drew her still more closely in awful fear.

"Of course. The time-space relationship has been altered with her as well as it was with us. You may live happily ever after, my children."

Minott's face was wreathed in smiles and Lola, comprehending that she was in a new and strange land, but not understanding how, was glad. She had found her happiness, and, but for the ache that remained in her heart for her father, was content.

THE END

www.ingramcontent.com/pod-product-compliance
Lightning Source LLC
Chambersburg PA
CBHW030318180626
46810CB00003B/1133